A SINFUL SHORT READ

Theirs for the TAKING

A DARK & DIRTY FIX

SARAH JD

Many thanks to my Alpha & Beta Readers: Anoesjka, Melissa, and my alpha & proofreader Jen.

Dedication

To those who wanted more smut from me.

Here you go!!

Content Warning

This book is a dark heat short story romance that
contains subjects that maybe triggering to some readers
and is intended for mature audiences.
Reader discretion is advised.
Please read the list of potential triggers on my website:

https://sarahjdauth
or.com/content-wa
rnings

PLEASE NOTE:
This book is written in Australian English,

Theirs for the TAKING

A DARK & DIRTY FIX

1

Ella

My hand trembles as I hover the pen over the dotted line, and I glance up to meet the House Master's analysing stare. My cheeks heat as judgement flicks over his expression, and I clear my throat, offering him a tight smile before glancing back down at the contract.

"Is there a problem?" he asks, his voice holding a rasp that sounds like it hurts.

"No," I say quickly, shaking my head and taking another quick glance at the papers.

The Mask House Auction Contract is fairly straightforward.

Signing puts me on tonight's list to be auctioned. Sold to the highest bidder. It's what this high-end sex club is all about. Women or men offering themselves for one night and walking away in a better financial position.

It's a club where identities are masked, and consent is contract-bound.

I've never done anything like this before, and I honestly never thought I would. But *they* are in town. The men that want me dead, so I need a cash injection, and I need it fast. Then, before the sun even rises, I'll take the money, pick up my pride off the floor, and run.

Scanning over the Anonymity Clause, my heart pounds so hard with each line I read, I fear it will beat a path right through my ribs, muscle and flesh.

No names or personal details are to be shared. Masks are to stay on at all times outside the private suites.

All acts must stay within pre-agreed boundaries, and safewords must be in place. Consent can be revoked but emotional regret holds no claims for complaint.

A knot twists my gut...

Maybe this was a bad idea. Maybe I'm better off robbing the Seven Eleven.

Shit. Maybe I should have just signed without reading it.

I bite back a groan.

Get a grip, Ella. Quit spiralling. How bad can it be?

That's when my eyes spot the words 'Ownership Period' and a cold spike of panic surges through me.

Ownership? What the hell do they mean by *ownership?*

Upon final bid, the seller is contracted
exclusively to the buyer(s) from 12:00 am to
6:00 am within a private suite.
During this time, the seller agrees to
remain accessible, responsive, and obedient
to reasonable commands, within the
boundaries of mutual consent.
Any breach of suite confinement will result
in security intervention and permanent
blacklisting.

Great. So sneaking off like a coward is out of the question. I'll be someone's *'possession'* for the night.

Skimming lower, I ignore the impatient sigh that falls from the House Master to spot words like consent, boundaries and punishments.

Punishment.

PUNISHMENT!

Jesus, I knew there'd be kink in the mix, but what kind of punishment are we talking here? Nipple clamps? Hot wax? Whips?

My body tightens at the thought.

I'm no virgin. I've been with plenty of men... okay so I've been with *five* men, but still, that's something. And yes, two were as vanilla as they come, but the other three... they weren't exactly gentle as they shared me.

Shit... is it hot in here?

Don't think about them, Ella.

Jesus, it's hard not to think about them when I think about sex. I just have to remind myself that they want me dead. If they catch me, my life is over.

"Miss, is there a problem?" The Master's scratchy voice shakes me out of my thoughts, dousing me with an invisible bucket of cold water.

"Uhhh, well..." When my eyes flick up from the contract again to see how annoyed he is by my stalling, I decide to keep my concerns to myself.

It's just one night. I need to do whatever it takes, get the money, and leave this town.

"No, everything is fine," I lie, forcing a smile. "I just want to make sure I understand my role."

"Very well," he grunts, gesturing for me to continue, so I scan over the NDA, and payment terms.

Opening bids start at twenty-five grand.

It's enough to get me far away from here, so I can start over... again.

The last section is called the *Disclaimer of Emotional Consequence.*

Just the heading has my stomach knotting up again as I scan the key points.

The Mask House is not liable
for emotional damage, psychological
entanglement, obsessive attachment, or
unintended consequences of auction
outcomes.
All bodies are purchased as-is.
All feelings are assumed at your own risk.
By signing this agreement, the seller confirms
they enter willingly, knowingly, and without
duress.

"Look, love, if you wanna do this, you gotta sign now," the Master huffs, clearly tired of my stalling. "Your lot is up next."

That disclaimer is a red flag if I've ever seen one, yet I nod and press my pen to the dotted line, signing my life away.

Before the ink even dries, the contract is snatched away, a door swings open, and the Master hands me off like I'm luggage, getting pulled into a bustling space at the side of a stage.

"Hey!" I gasp in shock as a woman snatches my wrist, hauling me towards the wings.

"Usually, people book their slots in advance and sign the damn contract straight away," she gripes, giving me the once over. "I'm surprised the Master even accepted you."

"What's that supposed to mean?" I squeak, glancing down at myself to see if there's something wrong with the way I look.

"It means your lack of organisation has a domino effect, darlin'," she snaps, fluffing my dark curls. "Why'd it take you so long to confirm your slot?"

"I had my reasons," I mutter, not willing to tell her it was a rash, last-minute decision.

"Robe off," she barks in a hushed tone, as a man on stage wraps up the bidding for a woman already out there wearing nothing but a black thong.

Before I even blink, my robe is off, leaving me in only my red lace bra and panties, and goosebumps scatter across my skin.

"You were smart to wear red," she says like she's not staring at my practically naked body before she starts rubbing some kind of oil over my legs and hips.

"Why?"

"Red is the colour of sin, darlin'. The men here like that."

My heart leaps into my throat as my gaze darts over my shoulder towards the door I was rushed through.

Maybe I can make a run for it? Just leave town with my one hundred and seventy-two dollars and my half tank of fuel. See how far I can get and figure out my next steps then.

"Next up," a deep male voice announces through the speakers, "a treat you won't want to miss!"

The woman at my side curses under her breath as she quickly finishes rubbing oil over my skin.

Wait... did she rub glitter on my skin?

Why am I sparkling like an oversized Christmas ornament?

"Please welcome to the stage... Erotic Ella!"

My stomach plummets.

Erotic?

That sure as shit isn't me.

"You're up," the woman hisses, quickly slipping a mask over my face before shoving me towards the stage.

Every instinct in me screams to spin around and bolt for the door, but before I even take another breath, a sharp slap to my arse sends me stumbling out onto the stage, and straight into the spotlight.

JELE

2

Ella

Sweat beads across my forehead under the harsh stage lights, my body fixed in place on the taped cross in the middle, like a target. Beyond the light, all I can see are the dark shapes of men in the crowd, sitting in the shadows while I'm on full display in the only lingerie I own. A red lacy bra and matching panties.

My hands are still shaking, so I clasp them in front of me to give me something to do, and when the masked auctioneer tells me to turn, I ball my hands to hide the tremble as I slowly spin.

I'm actually grateful for the mask. Grateful for the false sense of anonymity. Like I can somehow hide.

Sure, they can't see much of my face, only my red painted lips and my blue eyes blinking behind the mask. But what they can see a lot of is my body, which is exactly why these men are here. They only care about what it looks like, and what they can do to it.

My stomach rolls.

Shit. What have I done? This is a bad idea. The worst one I've ever had!

Facing the front again, I contemplate bolting off the stage.

Would they stop me? That woman? The Master? The security?

The lights slowly dim just enough to give me a better look at the crowd. There are too many shadows to count, all here to bid on women like they're buying art.

My mouth goes dry, and for a moment, I worry I might stumble across someone I know.

Like my boss at the medical clinic. He's rich enough to be here tonight.

Stop! Don't think about it, Ella. Think of the money.

"Thirty thousand!" a deep voice shouts, and my breath catches as my eyes dart in the direction it came.

"Our men are eager tonight," the auctioneer laughs, before opening up for more bids.

I thought I'd be lucky to hit the reserve price, but the room suddenly explodes with bids, voices calling from every direction, too fast for me to track.

With each bid, my eyes flash in that direction, but I can't make out who's fighting over me.

The voice in the back corner outbids as soon as someone else does, his deep tone clipped with a level of possessiveness that sends a ripple up my spine.

"Eighty thousand," someone else shouts, but my attention stays fixed on the back corner, to hear him up-bid again.

This is crazy.

"Ninety thousand dollars!" a man up front yells, before the voice in the back corner outbids him again.

"Ninety-five," he growls, like the other bidders are pissing him off.

I suppose they are, but I'm all for them up-bidding each other. I get eighty percent of the sale. This much money will help more than anyone here can comprehend.

The audience falls silent after that last bid, and the auctioneer does his thing, trying to convince someone to out-bid the last, and finally the man in the front gives in.

"One hundred thousand dollars!" He yells it like it's the winning bid, but the chuckles floating from the back corner has my breath catching in my throat.

Shit. There's a group of men in that back corner.

"One hundred and fifty thousand dollars."

Have you ever heard a room of men gasp?

No?

Well, I have. Right now, after the back corner guy drops a number no one would dare to match.

"Anyone interested in bidding higher?" the auctioneer calls, and when the room remains silent, he points to the back corner. "Sold to the gentleman in the back for one hundred and fifty thousand dollars."

My lips part in disbelief as hands close around my arms, ushering me off the stage and into the dark wings. My mask is pulled away, only to be replaced with a blindfold, leaving me blind and breathless.

"W-what's happening?"

"Bidder sixty-six requested his purchase be blindfolded," a woman answers as she steers me forward. "Come on. I need to take you to your suite."

A surge of panic hits me like a punch, my chest rising and falling quickly as I stumble alongside her.

I stupidly thought maybe I'd get at least a minute to catch my breath off stage. Maybe go to the bar and have a friendly drink with my buyer... my owner, before going behind closed doors.

"I think I made a mistake," I blurt, reaching for the blindfold, but my wrists are caught in a soft grip.

"Trust the process," she murmurs. "You might even enjoy it. The men who buy here are all about pleasure. And not just theirs."

I nod, hoping she's right as I fight back the sting of tears.

Think of tomorrow, Ella. Of getting out of here and far away from them.

I'm trembling as we walk, my ears opening up to hear anything I can since I can't see a damn thing, but with every step we take, the sounds of the club fade, and aside from our heels clacking on the timber floors, all I can hear is soft background music coming from overhead.

When the woman stops, I hear a beep and then a door opening, the timber floors changing to plush carpet under my heels as she leads me.

"We're in your suite," she explains, and I hear the door click shut behind me. "First things first. What's your safeword?"

"Uhhh, JELE."

"Jelly?" she asks to confirm, and I shake my head.

"It sounds like jelly, but it's JELE. J-E-L-E."

"Got it," she says, and I hear the squeak of a marker on a whiteboard. "Okay, let's get you settled. Your owner will be here soon."

Owner.

The word sends a shiver up my spine even as my stomach flutters with nervous butterflies. And not the good kind.

The woman guides me to sit, and I feel the softness of a couch against my legs, before she presses a glass into my hands.

"Drink," she urges. "It's Dutch courage."

"What is it?"

"The expensive stuff." She guides it to my lips, and I figure some alcohol is a good idea, because she's right. I need all the Dutch courage I can get.

I sip the chilled white wine, and then drain the glass, feeling its heat unfurl in my stomach.

"Good girl," she praises, taking the glass, and I'm about to ask for another when I feel something slip around my wrists.

"What's that?" I try to pull my wrists from her hold, but she holds firm.

"Your owner requested you be bound." She says it so matter-of-factly, like buying someone at an auction, keeping them blindfolded, and binding their wrists is just a typical day.

I guess to her, it is.

My lips part, ready to protest, when I hear a mechanical hum, and my arms suddenly start lifting over my head.

"What..."

"Relax," she soothes. "You can stay seated for now. Your *owners* will arrange you as they like when they arrive."

"Oh... okay." I trail off even though my internal alarm is screaming at me.

Run, Ella!

It takes me a moment of pushing down my panic for her words to sink in.

"Wait... did you just say *owners*? As in plural?"

"Yes," she answers smoothly. "Sorry. I wasn't allowed to mention that until you were secured."

"What?" My heart skips into overdrive, thrashing so wildly that I feel it's about to leap from my chest and out the closest window.

The woman doesn't respond.

"Why weren't you allowed to mention it until now? What's happening?"

Still, no answer.

"Hello?"

The click of the door opening and closing has me stiffening, and I force my ears to hear past my raging pulse to listen for other sounds in the room. But shit. There's nothing.

The woman just left, and now I'm alone, strung up like a prisoner, waiting for my *owners* to arrive.

Shit. Shit. Shit.

I tug my arms, but my wrists don't budge from their bindings, and I realise I really am fucked. There's no way out of this now. I just have to wait for my owners to arrive and have their way with me.

Shit.

Their... My body flushes as my mind goes back eight years. To a time I felt so worshipped, so alive, that I should have known it wasn't real.

But it felt real. *They* felt real. What we had felt real.

Since I can't escape this now, I summon the *me* I was back then. Willing to take risks. Curious as hell. Open to new experiences. She was sweet to most but wild to a select few, and right now, I need to channel her.

Slowly, my heart starts to calm, the rapid pulse in my ears quietens, and my body starts to heat as I remember them tying me up and having their way with me.

Anticipation has me melting into the cushions as my body starts to hum at the building need coursing through me.

And then I hear a beep, and the door clicks open.

JELE

3

Luey

Finally. There she is. Right where she belongs. She thought she could run from us. She should've known better.

We weren't unforgiving when we were seventeen, and the eight years since certainly hasn't made us any fucking softer.

Our gazes burn into our little Ell-Bell, bound to the overhead bar like our prize, just waiting to be claimed. Her arms are stretched up, her tits straining against the red lace of her bra, her head darting from side to side as her breathing quickens.

"H-hello?"

Fuuuck. That voice. I fucking missed it. Missed those plump lips and how swollen I know they can get after we've had our way with them.

Joel elbows me, gesturing to the whiteboard on the wall where her safeword is written.

Shit.

JELE.

My brows fucking arch at the tag we used when we were teenagers.

J for Joel.

E for Elliot.

L for Luey.

E for Ella.

Joel shoots me a wicked smirk and shrugs off his jacket before rolling up the sleeves of his shirt.

"If he kills her, that's on you," Elliot whispers beside me, and I roll my fucking eyes.

"You knew this day would come," I snap quietly so Ell can't hear, slipping off my jacket. "Don't fucking pretend you don't want to make her bleed, too."

I don't bother waiting for Elliot's response. I know how much he's ached for this day to come.

"Who's there?" she calls, her trembling doing wonders to the way her tits strain towards us, and a low chuckle rumbles from my chest at seeing and hearing her fear.

Fuck, she looked pretty on that stage, but now, close up, she's breathtaking. She's no longer the teenager we last knew. She's a woman. Her curves are voluptuous. Her voice is sensual. But I bet she still fucks like a wildcat.

Our little Ell-Bell sure is fucking lucky it was us that won her, and not any of those creeps still whining like little bitches about not winning the new piece of arse on stage tonight.

Not that we have any intention of going easy on her. She fucking ran from us, and it's taken eight fucking years of searching to find her. She's going to fucking pay.

The Mask House is a secret haunt for powerful men with kinks too raw for the outside world. Membership isn't cheap, but money talks. We'd heard whispers about this club for years, but never thought we'd actually come here. So imagine our surprise when we arrive in this part of the country to speak at a convention, and fate fucking delivers.

Our PI finally tracked down Ella, which led us here to this auction.

Sure, I paid one hundred and fifty large to buy her, but our rushed three-mil membership approval fee with a little extra hush money to ensure the cameras remain off will be worth it.

Ella has always been ours, and running from us will never fucking change that.

"H-hello? Who's there?" she asks again, and I briefly meet Joel's and Elliot's eyes before answering.

"Your owners are here," I growl, stepping closer, and fuck, my cock jerks to life when a whimper slips past her lips.

Has she recognised my voice already?

Leaning in from one side, Joel gets up close to Ell, and since she can't see, she has no idea that he's right there. "Do you know *who* we are?"

Her head whips in his direction as another whimper escapes her plump red lips.

I glance at Elliot, curious to see if he'll slip right back into the role he played so fucking well eight years ago. The quiet observer... until he snaps.

His jacket is off now too, his gaze locked on her as he moves past me like a predator that's finally cornered his prey.

"Ell-Bell," he whisper-sings eerily. "Ell-Bell."

Her sharp gasp is like music to my ears as her head shoots blindly towards Elliot, not even realising how close he is.

"E-Elliot?" she stammers, and Joel cackles at her fear on her other side.

"Still remember us, Elly-Belly?"

"No! Stop!" she yells, but there's nobody coming to help her. She's ours now, to do with as we please.

"Mmmm, you smell good enough to eat," Joel taunts, leaning so close I can tell by the way she stiffens she can feel the heat of his body.

"JELE!" she screams, and in unison, the three of us laugh.

As Elliot and Joel sink onto the couch on either side of her, I kneel in front of her, boxing her in, and adrenalin hums through my body as I take in every inch of her silky skin, a shimmer of glitter coating it, making it appear more luminous.

It's not enough to hide her scars, though.

The jagged one on her thigh from when she fell from the treehouse when we were kids. The tiny nick under her lip from the fist fight she got in with some chick that hit on me when we were teens. Even the faint scar on her ribs that matches the ones we all wear, self inflicted with the letters from our tag.

JELE.

And then there are the new ones.

A few silvery stretch marks and little surgical nicks low on her belly. All new chapters of her story we weren't there for.

That fucking reminder sends a rush of anger through my veins, and I grit my fucking teeth.

We should have been there for every fucking mark!

"You can scream your safeword all you want," I rasp, leaning in until my breath ghosts across her trembling thighs. "It means nothing here, Ell-Bell. You know you don't really want us to stop."

"L-Luey?"

Ahhh fuck, hearing my name on her lips like that, all scared yet familiar. Like she knows she doesn't trust me, but her body has other ideas.

Sliding my hands up her thighs, I urge them apart, and she resists, just like I expected, locking up like she still thinks she can fight me.

"No, stop." She tugs on the restraints overhead, trying to kick out her legs, but I wrap my hands around them, holding them in place.

"Uh, uh. We own you now," I remind her. "We've come to claim what's ours."

When she squeezes her legs tighter, I don't need to say a word. Elliot and Joel move as one, hands gripping a thigh each and spreading her open for me.

"Please. Wait," she gasps. "I never meant to betray you."

Already fed up with hearing her sweet trembling excuses, I fish the tape from my pocket, tearing a piece off, and slap it over her mouth.

Her muffled protests only fuel my hunger, and I decide it's high fucking time I finally get a taste of what I've been missing every single day since she ran.

Tossing the tape aside without a second thought, I drink in the sight of her strung up and open for me, her chest heaving, those tits, bigger than I remember, arching towards me like a fucking beacon.

Even the sight of my two closest mates on either side of her has me fucking hard. Their eyes aren't on me, but on her as they wait for me to start. Their fingers biting into her thighs, giving me access to the patch of lace covering her pretty pussy.

Hooking my fingers into the fabric, I quickly tear it at each hip, baring her in an instant.

And there it is, her slick, needy cunt, wet despite her protests.

"You filthy little slut, Ell-Bell," I growl. "You're already dripping for us."

Her muffled whimper vibrates against the tape as Elliot's and Joel's dark laughter rumbles through the room.

I can't hold back any longer, leaning in and slowly running my nose up her inner thigh until her scent hits me like the purest form of cocaine.

With an animalistic snarl, I bury my face in her cunt, sliding my tongue up her seam, and latch onto her clit with desperate suction, reminding her that she will always belong to us.

JELE

4

Ella

This can't be happening. My thoughts splinter into a thousand pieces as Luey's mouth claims my clit like he remembers exactly how I used to like it.

I try to fight it. I swear I do, but having them here, using me the way they used to, shatters my resolve.

Luey's tongue owns me, always the first to take control out of the three of them. The leader of the pack.

"That's it, Ell-Bell. Doesn't that feel good?" Elliot's soft murmur matches his caring soul, always the one to stand back and watch with the type of patience that is actually more of a self-inflicted torture, holding himself back until he can't take it anymore.

And Joel... shit, Joel is pure wickedness. He lives to sin. To experience pain, both to feel it and inflict it. He's the one who first showed me that pain could make pleasure burn brighter.

Together, the three of them are my kryptonite.

"Fuck, Ell-Bell. Make sure you cream all over his face so you can lick it off after." Joel's voice is a dark rasp against my ear before his teeth sink into my lobe, hard enough to sting.

I cry out, but it's muffled behind the tape, and the moment Luey brings his fingers up to graze between my thighs, I forget all about the pain.

God, yes. Please put them in. Fill me.

No, stop, Ella!

I shouldn't be thinking like that. I don't want this. I—

Another whimper gets cut off by the tape as Luey's fingers slide through my folds, his tongue unrelenting as it lashes over my clit while he sucks at the same time.

I arch, chasing his fingers, needing them inside me. To fill me. To stretch me.

"That's our good girl," Elliot whispers in my other ear. "Give in and take it all, Ell."

I thrust against Luey's face, and he finally rewards me by sinking two digits inside me.

My muffled moan is unmistakable, and tears spring to my eyes as I give myself over to them.

I was so stupid to think I could ever hide from these guys. To run from them. To keep my secret locked away.

I know they might kill me. Bleed me dry for betraying them the way I did, but hopefully, when they find out the truth, even if it's too late, they'll do the right thing.

"Fuck, Ell-Bell. You should see this." Joel nips at my neck, his teeth grazing against my skin. "Your cunt is already swollen and we haven't even begun to abuse it yet."

This time, he moves to my nipple, biting through the lace, and my whole body shudders as my pleasure builds at a startling rate.

"Take her tits out," Elliot rasps, I assume to Joel since Luey is a little busy right now, and I brace myself knowing Joel won't be gentle.

I wish I could see them.

Shit, no.

No, you don't, Ella. You wish none of this was real.

The cold kiss of steel glides between my breasts, and even though I should be shrinking away, I arch into it, desperate for Joel's pain. He always makes me hurt so good.

Yes. Please. Cut me.

"Christ, Ell. You haven't changed a bit, have you?" Joel breathes against my ear as he drags the blade lower, and with a sharp rip, I feel the lace give way and fall to the sides, my heavy breasts spilling free.

"Fuck, baby." It's Elliot this time, breath hot against my cheek. "Your tits are fucking huge. Look at those stretch marks. That's the sexiest thing I've ever seen."

I whimper, my tears finally falling, soaking into the fabric of the blindfold.

I wish I could go back in time and refuse Luey's arsehole dad and his threats. I wish I'd been strong enough to fight him. Call his bluff and hope for the best.

But I hadn't been back then, and I've been running ever since, knowing they were looking for me. Hunting for me.

They made a spectacle of it, too, plastering their search for me all over their social media. They even designed a game about hunting a woman who betrayed three men.

That game was about us. That game made them richer than Luey's dad could ever hope for.

I guess he got what he wanted. His son focused on making his first million. Something I would have distracted him from, apparently.

Instead, I ran, terrified Luey's dad would follow through on his threats, not just to me, but to Elliot and Joel too.

So I watched from behind a screen, moving as far away from them as I could without leaving Australia, my heart always with them even though they hated me.

My tears burn hot as some of them escape the blindfold, and the moment both Joel and Elliot latch onto a nipple each, I have no choice. I let myself go.

Joel's teeth are unforgiving as they bite on one side, while Elliot's tongue is a sinful contrast, sending me soaring.

The silk of Luey's tongue is relentless between my legs, and when he hooks his fingers inside me, hitting that sweet spot, every day of fear, pain, and loneliness I've felt over the last eight years explodes into a shattering orgasm that rips my soul apart.

I forget to breathe through it, barely register coming down from the high, in some sort of catatonic state when I realise I'm slipping into a dark pit of nothingness, and there's no way to stop myself from blacking out.

JELE

5

Joel

Luey and Elliot barely have Ella spread across the bed before I'm naked and crawling up her body, my restraint fucking gone.

"You wanna wait till she's awake?" Luey chuckles, amused by my lack of patience.

"Fuck no," I growl, white knuckling my throbbing cock. "She always loved it like this. I'm gonna remind her exactly what she's been missing."

"She's been crying," Elliot murmurs, tracing his thumb across her damp cheek, before popping it in his mouth with a low hum. "I always did love the taste of her tears."

"Not as much as I missed the taste of her cunt," Luey adds with a grin.

"You and me both," I grunt, lining up my cock.

Shit. This is it. After years of chasing a ghost, we fucking found her. Found out she was living across the other side of the country from us, and that tonight, she was auctioning herself.

It really couldn't be more fucking perfect.

"You need a hand?" Luey grins, like he knows I'm getting all fucking sentimental in my head.

"You wanna come cup my balls while I fuck her? I won't say no."

Elliot laughs, and Luey rolls his eyes, right as a soft groan floats up from Ella.

Poor thing passed out from her orgasm. Or more likely because she couldn't breathe properly on account of the tape over her mouth.

It's gone now. Blindfold, too, but her wrists are still cuffed and now secured to a rope on the headboard.

"Masks," Luey orders, tossing one to me, and I quickly cover my face.

She knows it's us, but this *is* the Mask House, and the masks will heighten the experience as she figures out who is who.

We're not brothers, but we often get mistaken for being siblings, so with masks on, it'll be visually harder for Ella to figure it out. Especially because she hasn't seen us in eight years.

We were boys when she ran.

Now we are men.

When another whimper falls past her lips, I can't wait any longer, driving the fat head of my cock into her slick heat in one brutal thrust.

"Fuuuck." I grip her thighs with pinching fingers as I bury myself deep, wanting to leave marks on her flesh.

My head falls back as her body adjusts around me, her pussy squeezing me like it doesn't wanna let go.

"She'll recognise your voice," Elliot warns.

"She'll recognise my cock," I grunt, slowly rolling my hips as she begins to stir.

She knows my brand of sex. Hard. Rough. Painful. So I give her exactly that, surging out and in, finishing each thrust balls deep with a sharp punch of my hips.

"Joel," she whispers, her lashes fluttering open.

There are a few long beats before reality crashes into her, those big eyes darting around the room, from my red mask, to Elliot's silver one, and then Luey's black one, before finding her arms stretched up above her head.

It's then that she reacts, her cunt clenching so fucking hard I nearly lose it.

"Fuck yeah, baby. Just like that," I growl, punching into her hard. "No one fucks like me. You remember how good it can hurt?"

She whimpers in response, so I lean down, sliding my hands under her, slipping my cock free and flipping her over.

Her gasp is heaven as her cuffed wrists strain, and I thrust inside her again, pounding her into the mattress.

"Who's fucking you, Ell-Bell?" I demand, parting her cheeks and spitting on her puckered rose before pressing my finger into her tight little arse. "Say my fucking name!"

"Joel!" she cries out, her voice trembling with raw need that has Luey fumbling with his fly to free his cock.

Elliot, always so restrained, watches, laying on his side, tension evident in the tight clench of his jaw, his hands balled into fists, as his hard-on remains tucked away under his jeans.

The fucker just watches, quietly torturing himself, as usual.

"Does Joel feel good, Ell?" Luey taunts, brushing a sweaty strand of hair from her face that is pressed to the mattress as I pound into her.

"So good," she breathes, her honest response taking me by surprise.

I was expecting more fight back. Perhaps a little fucking attitude, but no, she has already caved.

"Fucking hell, Ell." Luey roughly grips her jaw, forcing her closer to him. "You fucking left us."

"Yes!" she whimpers, her big eyes filled with tears as she peers up at him.

"Why?" he growls, curling his top lip like he wants to punch something.

"It doesn't matter." She tries to tug her head free of his grip, her voice laced with sadness.

Fuck that!

My palm cracks across her arse like a whip, the sting blooming red-hot on her skin, yet she fucking gushes around my cock, her slick cunt practically pulsing around me.

"If it didn't matter," I hiss through gritted teeth, fucking my finger deeper in her arse as my cock pounds her cunt, "then we wouldn't be here."

A strangled whimper falls from her this time, and I spot those plump lips quivering.

"Uh-uh," Luey snaps. "Don't you fucking cry, Ell-Bell. You don't *get* to cry. You're the one who ran out on us. Leaving nothing but a fucking note."

Fuck. The note.

I can still see her handwriting scribbled across the torn piece of paper, with the leather collar sitting right next to it.

'I'm sorry. I can't do this.'

"I didn't want to," she chokes out. "You don't understand."

"Then make us fucking understand!" I yell, my palm cracking across her arse again.

"Stop!" she screams, her face turning red before she breaks.

Right before our eyes, she erupts into tears, her sobs turning her into a blubbering, teary mess beneath me.

But still I don't stop fucking her. I don't even slow down.

If she remembers anything about us. She knows we don't shy away from conflict. We don't shy away from the painful stuff until it builds inside us that we can no longer hold it back.

Okay, well technically, Elliot can do that, but Luey and me? Yeah-nah, we don't do that shit.

Luey, clearly getting fucking impatient himself, signals for her to be flipped again, so I slip my digit from her arse, and my cock from her cunt, and flip her onto her back again, before slamming back inside.

"I can do this all fucking night, Ell," I promise, pistoning into her hard and rough. "You fucking know I can."

She whimpers, tears painting black trails down her face, her eye makeup already destroyed.

She's fucking beautiful.

Kneeling up by her face, Luey fists his cock with one hand and her hair with the other, guiding her mouth closer.

"Open up, Ell. Perhaps choking on my cock will help you to remember who owns you."

Doing the opposite of what Luey demands, she sucks her lips in, shaking her head.

She's never had a problem with choking on our cocks before, but maybe she's out of practice. Maybe she hasn't had a lover over the past eight fucking years that liked their dick sucked.

Reaching out, I pinch her nipple hard until she finally gives in and parts them to cry out, and Luey takes his moment and surges in.

His groan is deep and drawn out as Ell's lips wrap around his thick cock, and Elliot shifts to get a better view, his pupils nearly blown, fucking high on lust.

It does something to me, seeing him and Luey like this.

Watching Elliot torture himself, holding himself back, fucking edging himself like he doesn't think he deserves this sort of heaven, all while getting so aroused I just know what's going to happen soon, and fuck, I'm here for it.

And Luey? Fuck. He takes control of our girl so fucking well, reminding her who makes the rules.

Both of them, their reactions to Ell, her reaction to us, has me ready to nut.

Before we came to this club, the guys and I already agreed to no condoms tonight. Hell, at this point, getting her knocked up might be the only way to convince her to stay with us willingly, otherwise... well, otherwise she'll forever be our little prisoner, because we're not letting her go.

Not ever fucking again.

She's absolutely soaked, so I know she's not hating this. It's exactly how the four of us used to come together. Although we typically had her full consent. The lines are blurred as fuck here, and she may never forgive us, but fuck. I don't know if I can ever forgive her for leaving.

"Look how good you take my cock, Ell. So fucking perfect," Luey praises as he holds her head in place, thrusting so far down her throat that she keeps gagging.

And, fuck if that isn't the best sensation, her body coiling tight, every muscle tensing around my cock. It takes everything in me to hold myself back.

Elliot suddenly sits up, deciding to join in, but not for himself. For Ella. For me and Lu.

His hand slips down Ella's front, settling on her swollen clit, and the moment he starts working her needy bud, her moans mix with all the other sounds falling from her, making the sweetest music I've ever fucking heard.

"You feel that?" I hiss as I thrust, my grip on her hips bruising. "That's what you left behind. And that's what you'll *never* run from again!"

Her cunt grips me like a vice as Luey grunts, driving into her mouth and throat as she gags, tears pouring from her eyes. She tenses up, which has Elliot circling her clit faster, and she starts coming in a shuddering climax, milking my cock.

"I'm coming!" I roar, rocking into her one last time, throwing my head back as I empty myself so deep inside her it feels like I'll never stop. "Fuuuck! Take it, Ella!"

She shudders as she falls apart beneath me, and Luey throws his head back a second later with a savage roar, spilling straight down her throat.

6

Elliot

She stares at me, unblinking, curled up on her side. She's been in that position for over an hour, but her tears only dried up ten minutes ago, and she's been staring at me ever since. She hasn't bothered to look at Luey or Joel, who are both now partially dressed, having fed their cum into her pussy and mouth. Her eyes remain transfixed on me and the collar laying across my thigh.

Running my fingers over the leather, a thrill rushes through me at the thought of having it on her again. I fucking loved how she wore it for me. For us. No one knew why she wore it. They thought it was just her style. But we knew. We fucking knew it meant she was ours.

Ella clears her throat, and my fucking heart leaps in my chest.

"Are you gonna have your turn?" Her voice is husky, and all I want to do is go over there and kiss those pretty plump lips. Glide my tongue over them before slipping it inside and feeling hers brush against mine.

But as usual, I hold back.

"No," I respond, and she slowly shifts, pushing herself up on an elbow so she can see me better.

"Why?"

My nostrils flare at how fucking innocent she sounds. Like she didn't fucking destroy us eight years ago and every day since.

Don't yell at her. Don't fucking yell at her.

"You don't deserve that!" I hiss, slapping the collar hard across my thigh, not able to hold back any longer, and fuck, the burn of it feels so fucking good.

Ella flinches, not used to me losing my shit.

If only she knew I hang on a very loose fucking thread daily now.

"Because I ran?" she asks, already knowing.

"That, and because you still haven't explained why," I growl, leaning forward to rest my arms on my knees. "Eight fucking years, Ell-Bell, and you have nothing to say?"

Her nostrils flare this time as her cheeks heat in anger.

"Bit hard when I'm being choked on a dick," she fires back, and my lips kick up at her snarky remark.

"Luey's cock has been tucked away for an hour," I shoot back. "You've had plenty of fucking time."

She rolls her eyes. "Excuse me for needing a minute."

Luey and Joel smirk across the room, clearly happy about fucking her senseless, but she doesn't see, her attention solely focused on me.

"You've had more than a minute, Ell-Bell. And since you're required to please your owners," I relax back in the chair again, "to please *me*, tell me what happened. Tell me *why* things between the four of us were good... fucking *more* than good, and then all of a sudden you were fucking gone."

Her lip quivers as she finally glances over at Luey.

"If I tell you," she sobs as more fat tears burst from her eyes, "he'll take *everything* from me."

Luey stiffens, a frown tugging at his dark brows as he leans forward on the ottoman he's perched on. "Who will?" he asks, deciding to stand and move closer to the bed.

She stares at him for a few long beats, tears falling, sobs following.

"You know who," she snaps, and Luey loses his patience.

"No, I don't fucking know who, Ella. Who the fuck will take everything from you?"

Those glassy eyes dart to me then, followed by Joel who is eerily quiet, before returning to Luey.

She parts her lips, her gaze falling to the crumpled blankets on the bed, and she takes in a shuddering breath, like she's preparing to say something really fucking important.

"Your dad..." she whispers, her eyes remaining locked on the mattress.

All three of us frown at her words, knowing the only dad around at that time was Luey's.

"What the fuck are you talking about?" Luey snaps, closing the distance and taking her jaw in his rough grip.

"H-he found out a-about us," she whimpers, tears rolling down her cheeks as she looks up at him. "H-he had it all on v-video. The four of us together."

"So fucking what?" It's Joel that snaps this time, coming to Luey's side to tower over her.

"He s-said the f-four of us wouldn't w-work. Said I would put a wedge between you guys. That I'd have to c-choose." She shakes her head like she's picturing that day in her head. "Then he threatened me. Offered me a way out."

"Money," Luey snarls, shoving back from her and spinning to face the other way, his furious gaze now locked on me.

We've known for a while his dad had something to do with it, we just didn't know what, how, or why. When Ella first left, he had his men searching for her, or so we thought. And he'd even shown us bank records. Her bank records, with a large amount of money deposited into her account the day after she fled. It was a cash deposit, and he'd admitted that exact amount was missing from his safe.

We fucking believed him. Of course we did. We had no reason not to.

But Ella had never been about money before that, so taking it and running off never made sense to me.

"Yes, money," she sniffs, swiping at her tears. "Money to disappear..." she trails off, her big watery eyes flicking to me.

"And?" I urge, needing the fucking truth once and for all.

She stares at me for a long beat, pain flashing through her eyes before she starts shaking her head.

"I can't... he'll take everything from me."

"Well, you're off the hook from my old man," Luey snarls. "He died three years ago."

She frowns, those big eyes darting between us in confusion.

"But... I didn't see anything... I didn't hear anything."

So she *has* been keeping tabs on us.

"We kept it off social media," I explain. "Luey wanted to keep it quiet. Private."

"So you *were* stalking us." Joel smirks, and Ella shrugs.

"I had to make sure you weren't nearby."

"That how you found out we were in town?" I ask, starting to put things together.

"Yes," she whispers.

"And this place." I gesture around the room. "Why did you auction yourself?"

"I needed money to..."

"To run?" I ask slowly standing, and her eyes track the movement.

"Yes."

"Because you knew we'd been searching for you?" I take a step closer, watching her eyes fall to the collar in my hand.

"Yes."

"And you were afraid that we'd do what, exactly?"

Her lip trembles again, those big eyes flicking up to me. "Kill me," she whispers, shifting her gaze to Luey. "Do what your dad said he would."

I stiffen at that, and my gaze flicks to Luey and Joel to see them ramrod straight too.

Why the fuck would Luey's old man threaten to kill her? Just to keep her away from us. That doesn't make sense.

"Why would he say he was going to kill you?" Joel asks what I'm thinking. "Video footage of the four of us together hardly seems worth enough for something as drastic as that."

Her beautiful big eyes drop, a telltale sign she is still hiding shit from us.

"I have to agree with Joel," I grunt. "Why would Henry care about a sex tape of the four of us? Was he that much of a homophobe?"

"I don't think it was that." Luey speaks up. "I think he thought he was protecting us. He'd promised your parents that he'd look out for you both." Luey looks from Joel to me. "He thought she wasn't good enough for any of us. Had it in his head that she would ruin everything he'd built."

"You knew?" Joel snaps, and Luey nods.

"He told me on his deathbed."

I frown at Luey, but he avoids my gaze, so I can't tell what the fuck is really happening.

Fuck.

When mine and Joel's olds died in a helicopter accident, Luey's dad took us in. Treated us like his own sons. Unfortunately, that wasn't always good. He could be a cold man, and he expected us to work for him, like we each owed him something.

Sure, Joel and I owed him a lot for taking us in, but what the fuck did he think his own son owed him?

"You know what else he told me?" Luey snarls, glaring at Ella. "She has a secret. A secret he knew about. A fucking secret he took to his grave."

My brows shoot up as I stare at my best mate.

Is he just saying this to make Ella talk, or is this secret fucking true?

And if it is true, why the fuck has he been keeping shit from us... again? It's not exactly a surprise when it comes to his dad, but keeping stuff from us about Ella... Fuck. That doesn't sit well with me.

"What's the secret, Ell?" I ask, taking another step closer, and she sucks in her lips like she's sealing them shut. "You can tell us now, *or* we can have this conversation every fucking day from now until we die of old age."

Her midnight brows shoot up. "You only own me until 6:00 am," she rushes out, and the three of us laugh.

"We make our own rules, Ell-Bell." Joel flashes his teeth in a wicked grin as he leans forward to get in her face. "We own you for fucking ever!"

She flinches back, her eyes going wide as her gaze jumps from him to Luey, and then me. "No, you don't. What are you talking about?"

"It's time to come home." I grin, and she shakes her head vigorously, quickly shifting back on the bed like that small bit of distance will make a fucking difference.

"No. I can't."

"You can, and you *will.*" Joel kneels next to the bed, coming eye to eye with her. "Our plane leaves at eight."

"I can't." Her eyes dart to me, panic filling them.

What the fuck is she so scared of? We told her Henry was dead.

"You can." I grin, kinda liking her fear, knowing it'll be fun making her submit.

Her wide eyes flick to the door. She's gonna try to run.

Oh, *please* fucking try to run.

"Do it, Ella. I fucking dare you."

7

Ella

This room is generous in size, so there's a possibility I can get some space between me and the guys if I'm smart about it. But shit, let's face it. Clearly I'm not a smart person, or I would never have ended up in this situation in the first place.

If I wasn't so scared, I'd appreciate how lush this suite is. How it exudes class and luxury, even with the contraptions hanging from the ceiling, and the huge Saint Andrew's cross over in the corner.

Instead, this room feels like a cage. A prison. A place I'll never escape, even when this is over.

My gaze darts quickly over Luey, Elliot, and Joel and how their intense stares have my body reacting the way it used to when they all came at me like this. I was a goner back then, and I'm a goner now, only I can't be. I can't let that happen. I have to get out of here before it's too late.

Again, my eyes flick to the door. It's probably about eight metres away. If I'm fast enough, I might have a chance. I could run, forget about the money and just go. I'll just have to figure out the rest later.

I leap to my feet on the bed, faking to jump off in the direction of the gap between the guys, but at the last second, as they start moving to block that path, I dive off in the other direction, my bare feet thudding to the lush carpet as I run.

"Ha-ha! Yes. Fucking run!" Joel chuckles, his unhinged voice sending a shriek past my lips, even as I push my legs harder.

Just as I reach out for the door handle, someone crashes into my back, sending us slamming against the door, the chill of the cool wood startling me as my naked flesh is squashed to it.

"You're not going anywhere," Elliot growls against my ear. "You're ours."

A whimper escapes me as I blindly reach for the doorknob, not ready to give up yet. Elliot's weight against me feels crushing, his hands coming up to circle my neck.

Oh my God! This is it. He's going to kill me!

A scream rips from me as I struggle, his laugh meeting my ears as something snaps into place around my neck

"That's it, Ell-Bell. Scream for me like the good girl you fucking are."

Tears run hot trails down my face, their saltiness flowing into my mouth as Elliot's darker side comes out, his feet moving between mine to shift them wider.

"You're going to tell us your secret," Elliot rasps against my ear as he fumbles behind me, and a moment later I feel the tip of his cock press between my legs. "And then we'll make sure you never leave us again."

A strangled gasp gets trapped in my throat as he drives into me from behind, his hands bruising on my hips as he pins me to the door.

"This cunt is mine, Ella. I'm going to fucking love reclaiming it after dreaming about it for eight fucking years."

"Elliot," I sob, my face pressed to the timber as he pounds into me.

"You've missed this, haven't you?" he hisses, and a needy whimper escapes me, even though I try to hold it back. "Tell us your secret."

Shit. No.

"I can't," I cry, and he pistons faster. Harder.

"You fucking will," he growls, and a moment later, someone's fingers slide between me and the door, finding my clit.

Instantly, my body comes alive even as I try to fight it, and a moan escapes me as the fingers and Elliot's cock start to make me pliable.

"Yes," I half sob, half moan as my arousal clouds my mind, and Joel and Luey chuckle somewhere behind us.

"You were always the best at getting her to speak up, Elliot." Joel cackles.

"Yeah," Elliot agrees, punching into me, "I," punch, "fucking," punch, "am," punch.

Everything inside my mind ceases to exist. There's no more fear. No more worries. No more need to run. The only need I have is to give in to the quickly building pleasure coursing through me. Elliot's dominance, when he unleashes his true self, always speaks to my soul, and as fingers mash against my clit in a fast rhythm, and his dick hits deep, his commanding growl against my ear pushes me over the edge.

"Come for me!"

And just like that, I shatter, my insides pulsing around his cock so easily that I fear he and the other two were put on this Earth to own me, in every sense of the word.

"You're ours, Ell-Bell." Elliot pounds faster, panting as my climax draws out. "No more fucking running."

It's like he read my mind.

"I can't be yours," I whimper. "You won't want me when you find out..." I shudder, riding the last wave of my climax.

"That's for us to fucking decide," Elliot reminds me right before he stiffens, a roar of pleasure ripping from his lips as he finally comes, filling me.

J'ELE

8

Lucy

She's completely boneless as we secure the cuffs back around her wrists, before hooking them back onto the overhead beam. Gripping her hips, I hold on to her while Elliot and Joel run the support beam along the ceiling tracks, so she's left barely on her tiptoes in the middle of the room.

The setup in these rooms is fucking phenomenal. It's giving me new ideas for the room back at home that I've been adding to every month for the last few years with Ella in mind.

We are gonna have so much fucking fun in that room.

"Would you look at that beautiful sight?" Joel chuckles, and I follow his gaze.

Fuck. He's right.

His and Elliot's cum is oozing out of her cunt, making a wet trail down her thighs.

"Fucking oath." I agree with Joel. "Now I need to add to it."

Ella's head, which was drooping, slowly lifts, her red puffy eyes locking with mine as her top lip curls. "Your cum is in my stomach."

I can't fucking help but smirk. "I think I might fill every orifice. Remind you that you're our little cumdumpster."

"How could I ever forget?" she murmurs under her breath, but I fucking hear her.

Lurching forward, I grip her chin roughly, making sure her eyes are on mine when I speak.

"You must have forgotten eight years ago, or you would never have left us."

"I had no choice," she snarls, even as her eyes fill with tears again.

For fuck's sake. We are missing something. My dad wouldn't fucking tell me, and neither will she. It's driving me fucking insane.

"It's time to tell us your secrets, Ell-Bell." I lean closer, hovering my lips over hers. "Why did you steal the money?"

She scoffs, jerking her head back, loosening my grip on her jaw, so I release it, raising a brow as I wait for her to answer.

"I didn't steal the money," she snaps.

"My old man said you stole cash from his safe."

She laughs coldly this time. "I didn't steal it, Lu. He gave me that money to leave. Told me to go that day and never to speak to any of you again or he'd kill me."

I shake my head. "That doesn't make sense. Why would he do that?"

Her face falls, like her mind has been transported back to that day eight years ago, and when she speaks, her voice is small and timid. So unlike our Ell-Bell.

"I told you. He had a video."

"Nope." I shake my head, jabbing a finger towards her. "There's something else. What is it?"

She seals her lips shut, her eyes dropping to the floor as she retreats inwardly.

Shit. How the fuck do I get her to talk?

"You'll eventually cave," Joel snarls, getting in her face. "We'll spend every day from now on fucking you senseless until you tell us everything."

That gets her attention, her body stiffening as she shakes her head frantically.

"I can't go with you."

"Yes, you can," Elliot snaps from the corner, and her eyes dart his way.

"No, I can't!"

"For fuck's sake, this sounds like a broken record." I grunt, annoyed with fucking everything right now. "You are ours, Ella. That's all there is to it."

"No. You don't get it." Her voice rises like she's starting to panic. "I *can't* be yours."

My eyes narrow as I stare at her. "Why?"

Her chest starts rising and falling as her panic grows, those big dark eyes darting from me to my mates as fat tears burst from them once again.

"I belong to someone else."

I fucking stiffen.

"You have a man in your life?" Elliot darts forward from the corner.

"My PI didn't mention that," I snap.

"I-I do," she admits, and my heart fucking sinks as my eyes dart up to her hands. She's not wearing a fucking ring, but I guess she could have taken it off before she came here to whore herself out.

"What's his fucking name?" Joel snaps, and she answers immediately.

"Coby."

The room falls silent for several long beats.

Did she really just say Coby?

"What the fuck?" I snap, lurching forward and gripping her jaw again. "His name is Coby? Like our fucking dog? The one we all shared. The one we all loved and watched fucking die in the driveway when my old man accidentally ran over him?"

"Yes," she whimpers. "But the fact you still think that was an accident is perhaps the saddest thing about that, Lu."

"What the fuck does that mean?!"

"Your dad never liked Coby," Ella hisses at me, trying to wrench her head free again, but I hold tight. "He told you to get rid of the mutt every day. Said if it got in his way, he'd kill it. How can you ever think it was an accident?"

Pain I long buried rises to the surface as I stare into her eyes, so dark they are practically grey. I want to rant and rave. I want to lash out and make someone bear the fucking pain I feel. But instead, I bury it down, saving it for who really deserves it.

"It's time to forget about Coby," I say quietly, releasing her jaw again. "You're never going back to him. Ever."

"But... I have to. You don't understand."

"You know what?" I press my nose to hers as my own lip curls and I try fucking hard to hold in my rage. "I don't fucking care to understand. We own you. You're coming with us. That's all there is to it."

"But—"

"Put a fucking gag on her. I don't want to hear her excuses while we fuck her." I turn my back on her, and Elliot moves forward with a ball gag ready in hand.

Our Ell-Bell might not wanna make this easy on us, but we'll fucking match that. There's no way she's getting off lightly.

The guys take my cue as I start stripping again, their clothes disappearing just as fast as mine before we begin circling Ella like she's our fucking prey.

She fucking loved primal play years ago. Loved it when we chased and hunted her down in the woods surrounding my house. Most of all, she loved getting caught and being at our mercy as we fucking took what we wanted from her.

As Ella's chest rises and falls quickly, so do her plump fucking tits, so round and ripe, and bigger than they used to be.

Bet I could fuck them easily.

I smirk at that thought, fisting my cock and giving it a pump as we slowly circle closer, moving in.

She fucking knows what comes next. This isn't the first time we've had her strung up like this, and it won't be the last.

I fucking love seeing her black tears. How they dirty up her pretty, flawless skin, leaving gritty tracks.

There's a part of me that doesn't like that they are from crying. I prefer them from the strain of being choked on my cock. Of her body trying to reject it and gasp for air.

But for now, these tears will have to do until she can find the courage to tell us what we need to know.

Elliot stops behind her, and disappointment has my gut sinking. Not because he's the one that will get her tight arse first tonight, but because he's doing what he does every time he fucks a chick. The same thing he started doing as a result of Ella leaving us.

Taking her from behind. For eight years he's refused to bed anyone face to face.

Ella doesn't know this, of course. She just thinks he fucked her where he caught her before, up against the door, and she'll likely think nothing of him fucking her this way now.

"Are you ready for us?" Joel jumps in front of her, causing her to jerk in reaction, and he laughs before reaching out to roll her nipple between his fingers.

She gasps behind the ball gag, and Joel's smile widens.

"Yeah, you're ready to go down memory lane." He chuckles as he cups her tit, bending to claim the peaked nipple with his mouth.

A whimper falls past the gag this time, and her back arches, those plump tits straining closer to Joel as Elliot lathers her crack with lube.

Reaching around Ella's hip, I hold my palm up, and Elliot squirts a blob of lube into it before I slap it to my cock.

"Have you had more than two men at once over the last eight years?" I ask her, lathering my hard cock before giving it a squeeze.

Ella shakes her head, and even though she's trembling, I know she's not scared about taking the three of us at once. Her only fear seems to be related to her secrets and coming back home with us.

Too bad she doesn't have a choice in the matter.

As Joel swaps to her other tit, he shifts aside so I can get in nice and close.

My heart leaps as her fruity scent wraps around me, and I have to hold myself back from rushing this.

We all agreed the best way to remind her of how good we can be together is by doing it as a group, so I don't want to be the one to fuck that up by arriving too fucking soon.

Joel releases her nipple with a tug and pop, and she moans, not able to hide her pleasure.

"You like the rough stuff, don't you?" I ask as her eyes lock with mine, and I reach out, grazing the backs of my fingers down her wet cheek, and my beautiful temptress slowly nods.

There she fucking is. I knew our Ell-Bell was still in there. I just had to force her to come out and play.

I grin.

Peering over her shoulder, Elliot and I make eye contact, and he gives me a nod, silently telling me he's ready, so I reach down and grip her thighs, hoisting them up to open her to me.

"We'll make sure it hurts just the way you like it," I rasp as I line up the fat head of my cock, feeling the hot silk of her wet cunt.

Fuck. I've dreamed of this moment for eight fucking years.

Taking in one last breath to keep fucking calm, I slowly ease inside my girl.

Gritting my teeth, a groan falls from me as the feel of her molten moist cunt accepts me, squeezing my cock as I bury myself, inch by inch, into the only place that feels like fucking home.

No one has even come close to making me feel like this since she left. Not one single fucking chick.

Her breathing is rapid as Joel releases her tit and Elliot moves in close behind her.

I thrust inside her a few times as Elliot preps her arse, and I can feel his fingers moving in her back passage, lathering her up on the inside.

"Relax," he breathes against her ear, and Joel, always the helpful guy, slides his hand between me and Ella, finding her clit.

Another needy moan muffles around the gag, and her cunt becomes slicker as she relaxes.

"That's my good girl," Elliot rasps before looking down between him and Ella's back. "Here we go."

As I slide in and out, I feel his invasion from the back, and I suck in a deep breath as Ella squeezes me, and Elliot causes friction along my cock.

"Fuck yes, Ell-Bell!" Joel yells, overexcited as he drops to his knees to get a close up view of Ella getting dicked by two of us. "They feel so good, don't they, baby?"

Ella moans as Elliot starts easing his cock in and out of her arse, and we slowly work up a rhythm.

Having Ella in my arms again has me feeling more emotional than I thought I'd be, and as our eyes connect again, I desperately want to kiss her.

Her steely grey orbs flood with tears, and I know she's feeling the pain of whatever made her run from us. Whatever has kept her away from us.

"Are you ready to tell us your secrets yet?" I ask, and she sobs around the gag, her eyes pleading, yet she still shakes her head.

"You're a naughty girl." Joel hisses suddenly beside me, and her eyes flick to him as my pace quickens.

"You better get in her, man. I won't last much fucking longer," I snap.

"Fiiiiine." He groans, even as he wags his brows at her.

There's a reason Joel is the last to slip in. Not only is he flexible and strong, but he has a knack for contorting himself in the awkward position of being the third to bury himself in a chick.

He also has one fucking long cock.

He gets in nice and close next to me, more on Ella's side than anything, and I feel his dick brushing past my nuts as I keep Ella's legs hitched high.

"Ready for some DVP, Ell-Bell?" He snickers, pressing his tip into her already open pussy on account of my cock.

We all still while he feeds his cock in, my eyes shifting to Elliot to see his eyes roll in the back of his head as Joel's cock crowds us all in.

Whimpers fall from Ella, her head tipping back as she adjusts around us.

"Fuuuck, baby. This cunt was made for us." Joel groans, and as a unit, we all start fucking her senseless.

9

Ella

Sobs, whimpers, needy moans muffle past the ball gag in my mouth, and saliva drools out at the sides as I close my eyes and accept everything they are giving me.

God... I've missed it. Missed them so much.

I don't ever remember feeling this full, though. I think their dicks are bigger than they used to be because it both hurts and feels good. Kinda like the first time we did it.

My heart flips in my chest at that memory. It was the first time in years I felt alive. Like truly alive. And while I have felt alive since leaving them, I've never felt *this* alive.

I guess it could be because I haven't had three guys like this since I left them. Hell, I've only been with two other men, and they were so far in the opposite direction of what these three are that it's kind of funny.

But this. Ohh this. My arse has missed this. My pussy has craved this. And my heart... well, my heart has never been the same.

Joel is probably the most brutal with his thrusts, his body awkwardly positioned just so his dick can get inside me. His lips are pressed to my ear, his breath hot as he grunts with each thrust. And I tip my head onto his lips, longing to feel just a spark of his love, even though I know I shouldn't.

"Fuck, baby. You feel so good," he rasps, the vibration of his voice tickling my ear. "Do we feel good inside you?"

"Mmmm," I moan around the gag, and he nips at my lobe as he slips his hand between me and Luey again, finding my clit.

"Fuuuck, your clit is so swollen." He pants with each thrust. "Is it sensitive?"

I whimper in response, and he circles it, the pads of his fingers slipping over my nub easily with how wet I am.

"Do you love feeling Elliot buried in your arse?" Luey grunts, drawing my eyes to his, knowing this sort of talk turns me on even more, helping me visualise as well as feel.

I nod, not able to hold back the truth, while agony claws at my heart with the memory of how much it's hurt running from them.

I'll have to do it again, and this time, I don't know if I'll survive the heartbreak.

More tears and sobs flow from me as I finally let go, all of my emotions rushing to the surface with the rise of my pleasure, and I break for them. I break *because* of them.

"Let it all out," Elliot pants near my other ear from behind, his voice strained, although I get the feeling it's not just from fucking me...

Is his heart breaking too?

They pound into me harder, faster, and Joel's fingers are relentless, mashing my clit, sending me straight over the point of no return.

A scream rips from my throat as I explode, my head tipping back, my eyes squeezed tight as the most intense orgasm I've had since leaving them engulfs me. The pleasure-filled waves ripple on and on until I can't breathe.

Saliva pools in the back of my throat as the gag makes it hard to swallow, and I choke a little, filled to the brink, their pistoning dicks brutal as they each chase their own highs.

One by one, as I shudder around them, their own climaxes hit, roars ripping from each of them, and it's the last thing I hear before my hearing vanishes. Darkness rims my vision, and I know, without a doubt, that I'm about to pass out for the second time tonight.

I should fight it, but right now, I'm floating in bliss, wrapped in the scents of the three guys who have always owned my heart and soul.

Maybe I'm about to die, because I can't even feel my limbs. But I suppose if these three are here to kill me, I'd prefer this death to any other.

As everything goes black, all I can think about is how Coby will ever understand what became of me.

10

Joel

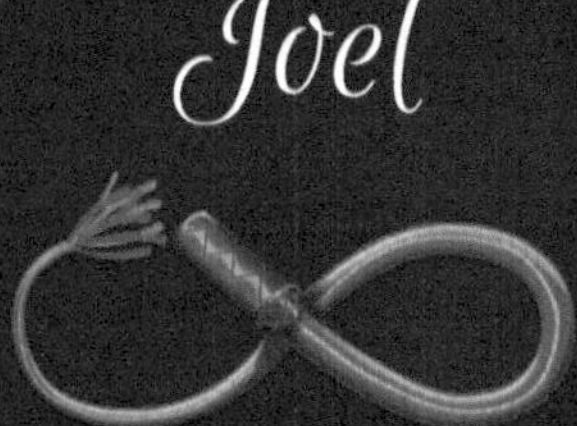

She's light in my arms as I carry her from the club out to our waiting car. I can't stop staring at her as I blindly follow behind Luey and Elliot as they lead the way.

Even with the dried black tears on her cheeks, she still looks peaceful like this, reminding me of when we were kids. When everything was simpler. When she used to sneak in through my window and curl up in bed with me, just because she felt safer there than in her own bed with her shitty foster parents.

That had been before the teenage hormones kicked in. We just saw each other as friends. Buddies. It didn't matter that she was a girl, and we were boys. It was always just the four of us, and we protected each other.

But we're not kids anymore. She left us without an explanation, and she made a life for herself on the other side of the country. She didn't even fucking care what it would do to us. She just took the fucking money and ran.

I don't know where the money is now though. Eight years ago, one hundred grand was a lot of money for someone her age. Given what our PI discovered, she hasn't led an easy life.

She works two jobs. One at a dry cleaner. The other waiting tables at the local pub. We have her address and a picture of the apartment she's been living in. If that's what you can even call it.

It's more of a box if you ask me, but apparently I'm a snob according to Elliot.

What can I say? I've gotten used to living in luxury with Luey's money.

Our Ell-Bell though… she hasn't been living in luxury at all. I bet that Coby fucker takes everything she has. I bet he's a fucking freeloading piece of shit.

Outside, the dawn air is chilly, but even the icy mist in the air doesn't rouse the beauty in my arms as we head towards the old-school chauffeured car.

"She's out good," Luey remarks as his driver, Martel, rushes to open the back door of the town car.

"Think she's okay?" Elliot asks, peering over my shoulder before I awkwardly lean into the back seat and place her up against the far door.

"She's fine. She's obviously forgotten her breathing technique over the years though," I mutter, securing her seatbelt.

"Her man mustn't be servicing her very fucking well," Luey hisses as I shift around and sit next to our sleeping beauty.

"Don't fucking talk about him," Elliot snarls as he gets in next to me. "He's a fucking dead man as far as I'm concerned."

Luey grunts in agreement as he slides into the front passenger seat.

"We'll get rid of that fucker and then get the fuck outta here," Luey snaps over his shoulder before turning to

Martel as he starts up the car. "Postpone the flight. And have a clean up crew on standby."

"Of course, Sir." Martel, always the loyal servant, nods, pulling away from the club.

Ella is wearing the clothes she came to the club in. Elliot fetched her things from her locker, so we dressed her as best we could after arguing if we should just leave her naked.

Luey wanted her naked and vulnerable, but I pointed out we have plenty of time for that, and the last thing we want is others seeing her creamy flesh and perky tits.

That's ours.

The House Master didn't bat an eye at the fact we were carrying our prize out of the club unconscious. Nor did he care that we took her things and left.

Next to me, Elliot rifles through her purse, like it holds all her secrets. "Why do chicks carry so much junk? Like what the fuck is this for?" He holds up a red plastic coiled band, and I snicker.

"That's a hair tie."

His brows shoot up. "How the fuck does that work?" He stares at it, stretching it a few times. "Looks more like something I'd use to bind her wrists with."

"Fuck... do you think *he* does that to her?" I mutter as my gaze shifts to her face, finding her eyes still closed.

"Dunno, but I might chop his fucking hands off before we kill him," Elliot snarls like he's picturing it. "Simply because he touched what's ours."

"Sounds like a plan," I mutter. "He'll fucking regret ever meeting her."

11

Ella

They're going to kill Coby!

They don't know I'm awake. I've been faking being passed out ever since Joel lifted me off the bed.

I've been reeling, trying to hold back my building panic with each word they spit about killing Coby. Will they really go through with it when they come face to face with him? Has the last eight years turned them into monsters like Luey's dad?

Ugh, he probably groomed them to be exactly like him.

So maybe the answer is yes. They really will kill Coby.

Cracking my left eye a fraction, I see the houses whiz by as we drive through the streets lit with the dull glow of the rising sun.

I know this area. It's my part of town. We are only a few blocks away from my apartment.

My heart flips, and not in a good way, my pulse kicking up as panic surges to the surface.

Shit. Shit. Shit. How do I stop this?

The car slows, coming to a stop at the traffic lights. There's a laneway just next to the road. It runs up through the next two streets and opens up five doors down from my apartment.

If I can get out and run, I might be able to beat them there since they have to drive right up the end of this street to circle around due to one-way roads.

But they could chase me on foot.

Fuck it. I have to at least try.

With my heart thrashing, I count backwards in my head from three, and the second I get to one, I open my eyes. One hand flies to the seat belt, unclipping it, while the other grips the door handle, pulling on it. To my relief, it opens, and I thank my lucky stars this car is old and doesn't have that function that locks all the doors when it starts moving.

"Hey!" Joel yells as I quickly leap out, his hand catching in my top, but the car starts rolling forward, and I start running, successfully breaking free from him.

From them.

I run like I've never run before.

"ELLA!" Joel yells, his feet pounding the pavement behind me, and my heart skips a beat.

Shit. He's going to catch me.

I leap over a rain-soaked cardboard box littering the path of the laneway, nearly slipping when I land.

Shit. Shit. Shit. I have to get away!

I just have to get home. Once I'm back with Coby, I can figure out what to do next.

I burst from the laneway, bolting across the street, barely looking for oncoming traffic since the streets are so quiet this time of morning.

"STOP!" Joel yells again, this time his voice closer, like he's right behind me, and a squeal lurches from my lungs.

"Hey!" A male voice comes from the yard lining the next laneway, and a burly looking guy steps onto the path.

"Help!" I scream. "He's trying to kidnap me!"

The man's fury is directed behind me, and I hear Joel yell a curse.

Risking a glance over my shoulder, I see the man stalking Joel, trying to grab him, and Joel tries to duck away, but the man is determined to stop Joel from pursuing me.

Part of me feels bad. I don't want Joel to get hurt, but shit, I can't let them take me.

So... I keep running.

Charging up the laneway, my stomach rolls with nervous tension as I get closer to my street.

My ribs hurt, a stitch behind them making it difficult to breathe, but I don't stop. I push myself harder, faster, desperate to get to safety.

Bursting from the end of the laneway, I turn up my street, heading for my apartment complex.

My apartment is on the ground floor, opening out onto the street.

I don't have my key, since my bag is back in the car, but my eyes find the ridiculous garden gnome Coby thought was top shit and had to be in our shitty little front garden, and I hurry for it, lifting it to find the spare key underneath.

I'm panting, and it's only now I realise tears are streaming down my face. I'm a total mess, but I don't care. I just need to get inside. Get safe.

With a trembling hand, it takes me three tries to get the damn key in the door, and as soon as it slides in, I unlock the door and hurry inside.

Closing it quickly, but quietly, I steal a quick glance in the mirror hanging crooked in the entry, and my eyes widen.

Holy shit. I can't let Coby see me like this. How would I ever explain? Dashing into the kitchen, I run the tap and splash water on my face, using the hand towel to wipe off the black smears of mascara as fast as I can.

The sound of a car pulling up outside my apartment has me stilling, my heart in my throat as I realise the guys are already here.

No...

Running from the kitchen, I bolt up the stairs, taking two at a time right as the front door crashes open, slamming against the wall.

"Ell-Bell," Joel sing-songs, his eyes finding me instantly at the top of the staircase. "That wasn't nice telling that man that I was trying to kidnap you."

He obviously got away from him, but he sure does look pissed.

"Please, don't do this." A sob lurches from my lips as I back up, while Luey and Elliot come into view, trailing Joel inside.

"You can't stop us, Ella," Luey snarls as they start moving up the stairs, slowly, like they are deliberately trying to appear calm, but the tick in Elliot's jaw is anything but calm.

I know that look. He's right on the edge, ready to explode.

As I step backwards on the landing, the floorboards creak, and I still.

Shit. I'm going to wake Coby. He always hears me when I try to sneak around, hoping he won't catch me.

"Is the fucker in there?" Joel snaps, curling his lip as they near the top of the stairs.

I shake my head.

Shit. I should just go with them. Maybe that way they'll leave without hurting Coby. Sure he'll miss me when I'm gone, but he'll move on over time.

"Stop," I hold up my hand as I whisper-yell. "I'll come with you, okay? Just turn around and go back downstairs. I promise I'll come with you."

Luey frowns, stepping around Joel as he moves up onto the top step.

"First, we deal with Coby. Then, we'll go."

My brows hitch as panic surges through me, but the squeak of a door opening off to the side has me stiffening.

"You okay, hun?" The female voice flows out from the door right before Margie's head pops out, her hair dishevelled.

"Y-yes, Margie. Everything is fine," I lie, and her gaze shifts to the three men towering before me.

For a long drawn out moment, Margie stares at the guys, never once questioning me, her focus on them, before finally flicking back to me.

"You sure?"

I nod quickly. "I'm sure."

She frowns, but even so, she quietly slips back inside her room, closing the door.

"Who the fuck is Margie?" Luey hisses quietly, his dark eyes darting from the now closed door, and back to me.

"It doesn't matter. Let's just go." I gesture back downstairs, but he simply smirks in that wicked way he does, and takes a step closer.

"Please don't do this. Don't hurt Coby. None of this is his fault," I plead, stepping back, my heels hitting the bedroom door.

"No more fucking around, Ella. Coby is a dead fucker." Luey snarls in my face, and I part my lips to beg again, but find myself shoved sideways, my knees crashing to the floor as Luey rushes for the door, the other two on his heels as he throws it open and storms in.

JELE

12

Elliot

I slam into Joel's back as he slams into Luey's, all of us stopping just inside the door. I mutter a curse, glaring daggers at the backs of my mates' heads when I notice them both staring.

Shifting around them, my gaze finds the bed, and a frown starts to crease my brow.

There's a bed. A single bed with dinosaur bedsheets, and in it, a little boy with dark shaggy hair is blinking his eyes open.

"Please! Don't hurt him!" Ella comes rushing in, barging past us, putting herself between us and the little boy.

"Who... who is that?" I ask, rubbing my eyes to make sure I'm seeing right.

Shit, did we do some fucking LSD or something?

"I'm Coby," the little boy answers for Ella, who glances over her shoulder at the little boy as he shoves the dinosaur sheets off himself and slips off the bed.

"Stay behind me, baby," Ella orders, but her tone is sweet. Loving.

Fuck.

FUCK!

THIS IS COBY!

"Why lie to us, Ell-Bell?" Joel grunts, his voice strained like he's trying to rein in his beast in front of the kid.

Her eyes are brimming with tears as she looks at each one of us, shaking her head as the little boy comes up behind her and pokes his head out beside her hip.

"This is why I had to leave. Henry found out I was..." she trails off, batting at her tears, her gaze darting down to her son's mop of hair. "He wanted me to get rid of... you know," she explains, her voice so soft and defeated. "I said I never would, so he gave me two options. To leave, or he'd..."

Kill her. Henry fucking threatened the life of her unborn child.

"This is the reason my dad paid you to leave?" Luey asks, and Ella nods.

"He had the videos. Said it was a scandal. That I didn't even know who the father was..." She shakes her head, her hand weaving into Coby's dark curls as he hides behind her. "I told him it didn't matter. That I loved all of you but he refused to believe it was possible. Said I'd destroy your friendship and reputations. So I took the money."

"You took the payout," Luey snarls, and Ella shakes her head, taking a moment to compose herself.

"Don't you get it, Lu? I didn't do it for myself. I never wanted to leave you." Her eyes jump from Luey to Joel and then to me. "Any of you. But I had to protect my baby."

Something starts burning in my chest, and it moves to my throat, and then the back of my fucking eyes, and I realise I'm going to fucking cry.

Because what the actual fuck!

Why am I about to fucking cry?

I stare at Ella. Her beauty seems more angelic than it did earlier, which makes no sense, but all I can think is... she protected our baby. She did everything she could to make sure he was safe, even if that meant leaving us.

"Ell..." I breathe, not sure what the fuck I want to say, but everything in me is screaming to rush over to her, pull her into my arms, and tell her everything will be okay.

But fuck. I don't know if it will.

Was Henry right? Is this little boy our kryptonite? Is he what will finally rip me, Lu and Joel apart?

I don't know if he's my kid, Luey's, or Joel's, but fuck, does that even matter?

We never had any qualms about sharing Ella. So why would we have any issues with sharing a son?

Fuck.

A son.

My eyes fall to the little boy peering around his mum, with hair the exact shade of Luey's, curls just like Joel's, and whiskey eyes... just like mine.

I gulp.

He stares up at us, not really looking scared, just curious about the three strangers standing in his bedroom.

What must we look like to him?

Shit... did he hear us threatening to hurt him? Why the fuck didn't Ella just tell us Coby was her son? We fucking thought she had a guy. A man that needed to be dealt with for touching what's ours... but this... this is something else entirely.

"I'm sorry," Ella whispers. "I was so young. I didn't know what else to do."

Pushing past Luey and Joel, I step up to our Ell-Bell, reaching up to press my palm against her damp cheek.

"I wish you had trusted us, Ell. We could have done something."

She shakes her head. "No, you couldn't have. We were all too young and powerless. Henry was in control of everything. There's so much you don't—"

"Mummy," Coby interrupts, stepping out from behind Ella, and my eyes fall to meet his as he looks up at me, and then behind me, to Luey and Joel. "Are these my daddies?"

YELE

13

Ella

We relocated downstairs to my shitty little living room, and I can feel them analysing everything as we walk through my tiny apartment. The mismatched furniture. The random throw cushions that don't match. The lack of luxury they live in every single day.

My legs are still trembling from my mad dash to run from them and their sinful torture. Torture I've missed for eight years.

I'm sticky between my legs, and I know I look as messy as I feel, but between fleeing from them and trying to get here before they killed my son, their son, there hasn't been enough time for me to clean up properly.

At the Mask House, I told them I couldn't tell them my secret, but now they know... one of them at least.

I watch each of them as they pull out a rickety chair at the dining table I found on the side of the road amongst someone else's trash.

It was my treasure, and a few nails were all that was needed to keep things together. It could probably use a paint job as well, but painting it has never been a priority. Not when needing to feed Coby is.

As they all sit quietly staring at Coby, he stares right back, his little hands resting on the tabletop as he waits for me to prepare his cereal.

I get to it, needing to keep busy, and as soon as I put the bowl in front of him, Joel speaks.

"Ahhh, any chance I can grab a bowl of that too?"

My eyes flick to his, and a grin pulls at the corner of my lips. "You still eat Coco Pops?"

He rolls his eyes. "Of course I still eat Coco Pops. It's not just for kids, you know."

Coby giggles. "Mummy says it's a kid's food, but sometimes I spot her eating a bowl when she watches TV after I go to bed."

I gasp, shocked he'd throw me under the bus like that, and the guys chuckle, finally starting to relax in their seats.

Well, everyone but Luey. He's far too uptight.

"You're a dibber dobber." I laugh at Coby, and he shrugs, not at all concerned.

When my eyes meet Joel's, he shoots me a wink, and I feel my cheeks heat, so I turn away and get busy pouring another bowl of cereal, followed by four cups of strong coffee.

We are going to need it today.

Coby chats away with the guys, telling them about school, and answering their questions, and with every passing minute, my heart starts to sink even more.

This was never meant to happen. Coby was never meant to meet his dads. They were never meant to meet him.

I know Luey said his dad died, but this whole thing still feels risky.

The guys have built their lives. They are public figures. They can't all of a sudden show up with a woman no one has seen with them before, and a kid that calls them all daddy, even though only one of them can actually be his dad.

I need to protect Coby, but now that the guys know about him, I get the feeling I'll need to loosen the reins. Share my son with the three of them.

"I take it this is them?" Margie mutters as she shuffles into the room, heading straight for the coffee.

My eyes dart to the guys, their brows raised, but I nod at Margie, knowing it's useless trying to hide anything from this woman.

"Yes, Margie, this is Luey, Joel, and Elliot." I gesture to each one, and she simply nods, already knowing about their existence.

I needed her to know about them in case they ever showed up randomly one day since she cares for Coby when I'm not here.

"I have a gun," she snaps at them all of a sudden, shooting them each a glare. "I won't hesitate to blow your little pin dicks off if you start shit."

I gasp, Joel chokes on his cereal, and Coby giggles.

"Margie, you said shit and dick. You owe the swear jar two dollars."

Margie beams at Coby. "So I do. It was worth every cent." She cackles as Coby giggles, and I'm left sighing as Margie moves to her purse and takes out the money.

"Who are you exactly?" Luey snaps, earning a raised brow from Margie.

"I'm the one who looks after your son when his poor mother has to work two jobs to feed the boy. That's who I am."

I expect Luey to cringe, or even start ranting about not even knowing Coby existed, but all he does is nod.

"Noted. Thank you for helping Ella in our absence."

For a long beat, Margie has a stare off with Luey before she nods and returns to her task of slipping the money in the swear jar. She doesn't say anything, but she doesn't need to for me to know she'll have a close eye on them.

"Come on Coby, let's get you in the shower. Gotta wash the stink off you."

"Ew, Margie." Coby giggles. "I don't stink."

"Sure you do. You have boy cooties. All boys have to shower each morning to wash away their stinky boy cooties."

Coby cackles as he rushes out of the room with Margie on his tail, leaving me alone with the guys.

I gulp, and my mouth goes dry.

"So he's ours?" Luey asks. "One of ours?"

I nod, staring into my coffee mug for a beat before looking up to see three sets of dark eyes.

"Yes. Biologically, he's one of yours," I say the words I never thought I'd have to say, but now that it's happening, it's a relief to share them. "I never found out who the biological father is because... to me..." I clear my throat thick with emotion. "To me, you're *all* his father."

There's nothing but deafening silence, and I reluctantly drag my gaze from my mug to find the three of them looking at one another like they can hardly breathe.

Joel looks terrified, Luey looks intrigued, and Elliot looks stricken... wait, no. Elliot looks more like he lost his puppy.

Luey's lip curls. "I wish my old man had the guts to tell me the truth back then, but he knew we'd choose you," he mutters, stepping towards me. "He made us his puppets. Poisoned our minds with hate for you. Kept us from searching for you for too long. Blocked every fucking lead we got to your whereabouts." Luey reaches out and brushes the back of his knuckles over my cheek. "I'm sorry it took us so long, Ell."

"Do you hate me?" I whisper, my lower lip wobbling. "For running. For taking your son away?"

"I've been angry for years. But I've never hated you. Not once," he rasps, leaning in to press his lips to mine.

I melt into him, brushing my tongue against his, missing this gentle side of this hard guy. Luey has always had to live up to his father's standards, but I suppose now he doesn't have to. If Henry is dead, then Luey is free to live life how he wants.

When Luey breaks the kiss, I see Joel and Elliot closing in.

"You told Coby about us?" Joel asks, and I nod.

"I wanted him to know about all of you." I glance back at Luey. "I ran from your dad, Luey. Not the three of you despite how it turned out."

A warm palm presses to the small of my back and fingers grip my chin, turning my head where I find Joel smiling down at me.

"Ours," he murmurs, and I melt against Luey's chest as Joel leans in to claim my lips this time.

God, I'm going to combust at this rate, letting Joel's tongue invade my mouth. I've missed the way he kisses. Like I'm the most delectable dessert known to man.

"Ella," Elliot rasps against my ear. "I need you."

I whimper into Joel's mouth as Elliot nips at my ear, and shit, there's about to be a full-blown porn scene in my kitchen.

I draw back from Joel, gasping, and ready to step away to get some space between us, but Elliot fists the back of my hair, turning my head his way, and claims my lips.

Ooooh. Elliot. He has a beast inside him. Kind of like Jekyll and Hyde, and when he lets his walls down, Hyde comes out in the most sinful way.

Someone cups my tit, and someone's hand skims down my front to palm my mound, and oh myyyyy, I want to give these men everything... But I can't.

Jerking back from Elliot's sinful lips, I gasp. "Wait!"

I somehow wrangle myself free of the three of them, crossing over to the other side of the room and hating that this place is so small because I've literally only been able to put three metres between us.

"Ell?" Joel asks, staring at me in confusion.

"You're making it hard to think," I blurt, and Luey chuckles.

"Well... yeah. You always loved that."

Taking in a steadying breath, I shake my head, trying to compose myself.

"Things are different now. I'm a mum. I can't just have a fucking orgy in my kitchen." I throw my hands up in the air. "Besides, don't you have a plane to catch? You have to get back home."

"Oh, I see what's going on," Elliot mutters. "You think since we now know your secret and who Coby really is that it changes why we are here. Well, let me reassure you, Ell. It fucking doesn't. You're still ours, and you're still coming home with us."

My mouth drops open as the other two nod at Elliot's words.

"I can't. Our life is here. Coby goes to school and—"

"Let me stop you right there," Luey snaps, his hard gaze locking with mine as he takes a few steps closer. "You went to that fucking club to earn cash fast, so you could run. So you could take Coby and leave before we fucking found you. Don't you dare act like coming home with us is a fucking inconvenience. You are ours, Ella. Coby is ours. We won't fucking leave without either of you."

"But Margie..."

"Bring her. We'll pay her to watch Coby. We'll give her a place to stay. Meals. A fucking better life than this." He gestures around him, and I flinch.

"Don't you dare turn your snobby nose up at the way I live!" I yell, my fists balling as I fight to rein in my anger. "You've never lived a day without knowing if you'll be able to feed yourself. You have no right to judge the way I live, or the things I've had to do to survive!"

"He knows," Elliot interjects, shooting his glare at Luey. "Right, man? You fucking know you don't have that right."

Luey simply grunts in response, but his hard stare never leaves my face. "You decide if you want the old bat to come or not, Ella. But you and Coby will be on that fucking plane with us. I'll fucking bind and gag you if I have to."

Anger flares in my cheeks, and I'm sure they're red as I snarl at Luey. "You wouldn't dare."

He quirks a single brow. "Wouldn't I?"

We stare at each other for so long, I barely hear the footsteps coming back down the stairs.

"Mummy!" Coby runs into the room. "Margie said we're going on a trip."

My brows shoot up, and I shake my anger away to focus on my son.

"She said what?"

"She said we are going on a plane with my dads." Coby jumps up and down in excitement. "Can we, Mummy? Pleeeeease?"

He looks like Luey right now. The drunk version of Luey when his expression is soft and playful.

I open my mouth to respond, but Joel beats me to it.

"Of course you can. You should probably pack a bag. Want some help?"

Coby nods. "Can my dinosaurs come too? They've never been on a plane."

My shoulders drop as Coby and Joel head upstairs, leaving me with Luey, Elliot, and Margie.

"Really, Margie?"

She shrugs. "I may have eavesdropped, and I'm all for relocating out of this dump."

I tip my head back and stare at the paint peeling on the ceiling.

Jesus. I should just give in. How bad could it be?

Shifting my gaze to Luey, I cross my arms over my chest, and a smirk kicks up his lips.

"Come on, Ell-Bell. Give in to me." He slaps his chest, and I roll my eyes.

"Fine, but you need to remember Coby is only a little boy. He needs attention. Like, all the time. I can't just spend the whole day..." My eyes snap to Margie, and she rolls her eyes this time.

"Oh, for God's sake, girl. Just say it. You can't spend all day fucking them."

I gape, and she waves a dismissive hand at me. "I'm going to pack."

"I like her," Luey chuckles.

"Of course you do." I realise this conversation is futile at this point, so I turn and head for the stairs. "I'm going to shower, and then to pack, I suppose."

"Good girl." Elliot praises as I leave, and Luey's chuckle floats up the stairs, making this house feel less empty for the first time ever.

I hurry into the bathroom, stripping out of my clothes and turning on the water.

I feel filthy, in the best way, but even so, I don't really like feeling like that around my son.

Getting into the shower that's over the bathtub, I stand under the steaming hot water for a moment, and think over everything that's happened in the last twenty-four hours. I certainly didn't wake up yesterday morning thinking any of this would have happened.

As I lather shampoo in my hair, I feel a cool breeze on my side as the shower curtain suddenly tugs open, and before I have time to gasp, a hand slaps over my mouth from behind.

14

Luey

Ella struggles against me for a few moments until she realises it's me and Joel slipping into the shower bath thingy with her.

This time, I'm taking her from behind. I wanna feel her tight arse strangle the fuck outta my cock until it milks me of every drop of cum in my balls.

"You didn't think we'd just sit out there twiddling our thumbs knowing you're in here naked, did you?"

She whimper-moans against my hand as I cup her tit and Joel moves up in front of her.

"Shhhh, Ella. You don't want Coby or Margie to hear you, do you?"

She shakes her head under my hand, and Joel grins wickedly before dropping to his knees.

"Remember, Ell-Bell. Keep quiet. Don't make a fucking sound."

She nods again, and I release her mouth, reaching for the lube and making quick work of lathering her arsehole up as well as my cock as Joel takes the brunt of the falling water.

On his knees, Joel lifts one of Ella's legs, hooking it over his shoulder, opening her up to him and me, and as I line up my cock with her puckered rose, Joel moves in and sucks on her clit.

She starts to cry out, but slaps her own hand over her mouth to muffle the noise, and I snicker against her neck as I push the tip of my cock in.

"Does that feel good, Ell?" I ask, and she nods quickly, reaching around to dig her claw-like nails into my hip, trying to drag me closer. "It'll be like this every fucking day from now on. You. Our toy to play with. To take whenever the fuck we want." I ease all the way in, and start to retreat halfway out again. "You won't say no. You won't deny any of us access to this body. Will you?"

"No," she breathes quietly, and as I peer down over her shoulder, past her perky tits, Joel's eyes lock with mine as he eats the fuck outta our girl's pussy.

"Fuck, Ella. Grind on his face," I rasp against her ear. "Fuck it until you drown him in your juices."

She whimpers just like I knew she would, my words always having that effect on her.

Our little Ell-Bell is a filthy thing. On the outside, you'll find beauty, poise, and class. But fuuuck, inside her dirty little mind, she's just as fucking depraved as us.

Her arse is tight and hot, and fuck, it's like heaven. I slowly pump in and out of her while my fingers play with her nipple, rolling it and pinching the tight peak until she quietly moans.

Joel moves in front of her, and I feel his fingers grazing over my nuts before giving my balls a little squeeze, and fuuuck, this prick knows what I like too fucking well.

He doesn't do it for long though, his attention on our Ella, and I feel his fingers slide inside her cunt.

A muffled cry falls past her hand, and I know he's hitting all the right places inside her. I used to think he was a pleasure Dom, but the fucker likes inflicting pain just as much.

The moment Ella's cunt starts to tighten with a frantic rhythm, I know she's about to come, so I pinch her nipple hard, thrusting faster, and breathing against her ear.

"That's it, Ell. Fuck his face. Grind that dirty cunt on him. Don't let him fucking breathe."

She shatters, a cry ripping from her as violent spasms take over her entire being, and I release her tit to slap my hand over hers, trying to double up on keeping her fucking quiet.

The moment her climax subsides, she goes slack, and Joel finally comes up for a breather, his tongue darting out to clean up around his lips.

"You taste like heaven, baby." He grins, coming to stand, his hard cock jutting out in front of him as he fists it and gives it a pump. "I could taste Luey's, Elliot's and my cum, as well as yours. Such a fucking delectable recipe."

I chuckle even as she whimpers again, and I know his words are already reigniting her arousal.

"You want this inside you?" He nods his head down to his cock, and she nods quickly behind mine and her hand. "You want more of my cum again?"

She nods.

"You want me to fuck you so hard that I'll make Luey come too?"

She nods, and I chuckle.

"Her tight arse is enough to make me come," I rasp, my voice a little choked from the strain of holding back.

Joel lifts a brow, a mischievous expression crossing his face. "I bet if I cup your balls again, you'll blow the tip right off your cock."

The fucker is baiting me, but fuck it, I'll take it.

"Go on then."

Joel chuckles, lining up his cock to Ell's cunt, and in one swift move, he surges in.

There's no fucking way everyone else in this apartment didn't hear our three combined moans, and I just have to hope Elliot is keeping Coby busy enough he doesn't decide to come looking for his mum.

Joel doesn't take it easy on Ell, or me, thrusting hard and fast, making sure each punch of his hips sinks his cock deep, and I feel every fucking stroke.

Gritting my teeth, I try to hold out. I'm not ready for this to be over yet, but Joel reaches down, in his awkward lemur ability, and not only cups my balls, but fucking tugs on them.

I'm helpless, the stimulation on my nuts and the way Ella's arse clamps around my cock, along with Joel's hard rod of a dick stroking it through the wall of her pussy, I fucking explode.

It's like a detonation, my whole fucking body shuddering so hard that I nearly lose my footing and fucking slip, but Joel, ever the fucking saviour, reaches out and steadies me, even while he keeps pounding into our girl.

I stay buried in her arse, wanting her to remain full, and it only takes Joel a couple more thrusts before Ella is following me in her own orgasm, and once her cunt starts kneading Joel's cock, he lets go and comes too.

"Mummy?"

We all stiffen at the sound of Coby's voice.

JELE

15

Ella

My heart stops... nooo. Please tell me I'm hearing things!

My eyes snap to the door to find Coby standing in the doorway, a blindfold covering his eyes while Elliot stands behind him wearing a shit-eating-grin.

"Uhhh," I squeak. "Coby... Mummy is in the shower."

"I know that. Duh." Coby throws his hands up in the air. "That's why I'm wearing a blindfold."

Luey shifts behind me, and I glance over my shoulder to see him smothering a laugh, and the cut off chuckle from Joel has me glaring in his direction as he nods in glee.

Jesus H Christ. His mischievous expression matches the one Coby gets sometimes.

"What do you want, Coby?" I rush out, trying to ignore the three guys and their amused expressions.

"Oh." Coby's lips kick up in a wide smile. "Margie wanted me to tell you that she's packed and ready to go, and if you don't hurry up, she's going to tell me the story about how you're a bird and my dads are bees and how they pollinate... or something. I don't really get what she's talking about."

That evil old...

"Okay, Coby," I say through gritted teeth. "We're... I mean, I'm coming."

"Literally." Elliot chuckles behind Coby, shooting me a wink right before he steers my son blindly out the door.

"Oh my fucking God!" I hiss as the door closes. "We need to set some boundaries. You can't just fuck me whenever or wherever you like if we come back with you."

Easing his softening cock from my tense arse, Luey chuckles against my ear.

"There's no *if*, Ella. You *are* coming with us. And if you recall, just a few minutes ago, you agreed."

"I did not," I snap, trying to shift away from him, but Joel presses in nice and close, keeping me pinned between them, his long dick still buried inside me.

"Oh, you did." Joel beams. "I believe Luey said it will be like this every day from now on. That you are our toy to play with. To take whenever the fuck we want." Joel's gaze flicks over my head to speak to Luey. "That sound about right?"

"You left out the part where I said she won't say no or won't deny any of us access to this body." Luey's hands glide down my sides, coming to rest on my hips as his lips start kissing a trail up the side of my neck.

"Ahhh, yes. That's right." Joel's brows lift before smirking down at me. "Then he said, *will you?* And do you remember what you said, baby? You said *no*. You agreed that you won't deny us. So, you see, we will fuck you wherever and whenever we want, and you'll be our good girl and do it. Won't you?"

Shit. I sigh, feeling more arousal build in me from the dominant tone in Joel's voice, and the way Luey is kissing me and... shit, and I can't deny them. I'm too weak to refuse them when they tell me what to do. When they control me.

"But, Coby..." I can't speak, because Joel leans down and sucks my nipple into his mouth, and I can't believe I'm turned on again.

This can't be normal.

"That's what Margie is for," Luey rasps before nipping at my earlobe. "Now get your sweet arse out of this shower and get ready. We have a plane to catch."

And just like that, both Luey and Joel stop seducing me and slip out of the shower.

Oh... my...

I swear these arseholes rehearse driving me crazy like it's an art form.

They leave me to finish up showering, and I do so in a numb state as I go over everything that's happened. It seems ridiculous to suddenly pack my things and get on a plane with these men and go back to the place we grew up. To uproot Coby and completely change his life.

But Luey is right. I was going to do that anyway by fleeing.

And would it be so bad? Coby would have nice clothes and new schoolbooks. He'd have more opportunities than I could ever give him.

And he'd have his dads. All three of them.

I pretend that's the only reason I accept that this is happening, and that it has nothing to do with the fact that I still love all three of them. That I've pined over them for eight years. That I've dreamed about them and longed for them to come and save us, despite how I betrayed them by taking the payoff from Henry.

They don't know everything though, and it needs to stay that way.

I may have been one thing that could have put a wedge between the guys, but I wasn't the only thing. I don't want them to ever find out that truth. It'll kill them. Destroy their friendships and everything they've built together.

Henry was right about that, but it had nothing to do with me, and everything to do with him.

He is... was... a monster.

I'm glad he's dead, and knowing that is the only reason that me returning with the guys is okay.

After showering, dressing and packing, I meet Margie and Coby in the tiny living room, and I'm about to ask Margie if she's really okay with moving, but she's the first to pick up her bags and hurry out to the second town car. Her eagerness is almost comical, and I have to assume she's more than happy to move across the country to Australia's east coast.

The guys are surprisingly professional as we travel to the private airfield and board the plane. Each of them is wearing jeans and a tee. Luey in all black. Joel in blue jeans and a red tee. And Elliot in blue jeans and a grey tee.

We are ushered from the cars to the plane, which is a whole other thing because I've never been in a plane like this. Small yet luxurious, with ivory leather seats and rich timber detail.

Coby is beside himself, bouncing in the seat like he has ants in his pants, and Margie happily takes a glass of bubbles from the hostess, telling her to leave the bottle.

Good grief. I knew Margie was no fuddy-duddy, but I think I've unleashed something inside her.

Luey sits down next to Coby and starts chatting with him, so I take a seat opposite, with Elliot and Joel on each side of me, and I feel like I'm having an out-of-body experience as I watch my son's eyes light up, looking out the window as the plane takes off and propels up into the sky.

I'm quiet. Observing everything. From how Luey, probably the coldest of the three guys, warms right up to Coby, pointing at things out the window.

My eyes fall to my lap as I fight a smile, emotions I didn't think I'd feel rising to the surface. My gaze flicks to Joel's hand, resting on his thigh, and then to Elliot's, doing the same as Joel.

I study each of their hands, now bigger and stronger, and a little aged. Joel has a tattoo that snakes down from his arm, over the top of his hand. It looks like dragon scales, and I wonder if it means something.

"You alright, Ell?" Elliot whispers against my ear, and I nod quickly, smiling a little as I glance up.

His whiskey eyes are bright as he scans my face, like he's seeing it in a new light and memorising every detail, so I take a moment and do the same to him.

He's grown into a handsome man. His dark hair is straighter than Luey's and Joel's, but he's grown it long, and it's a little shaggy.

It makes him look like a badass. Not something he looked like back when we were teenagers.

This version of him better matches the man inside though. Dark and broken.

"This has all happened so fast. It doesn't seem real," I admit, and the slightest smile stretches one side of his mouth.

"Did you really think we were here to kill you?" he asks quietly so Coby can't hear, and I nod, my cheeks heating with shame, because how could I seriously think they would ever do that?

Henry got in my head eight years ago, and I guess because I know the lengths he'd go to, I assumed these three would have been moulded that way too now.

I mean... they were determined to kill Coby when they thought he was my partner.

Maybe I wasn't far off the mark.

"Kidnap you, yes. But never kill you," Elliot rasps, hooking his finger under my chin and tilting my head back as he leans closer. "We could never truly hurt you, Ell-Bell."

My eyes heat, and I nod quickly, pulling back to get some space between us.

Falling apart in front of Coby isn't ideal, and Margie is across the aisle sipping on her drink watching me like a hawk, so I need to keep my shit together.

"I need to use the bathroom," I mutter, quickly unclipping my seatbelt and hurrying to the back of the plane.

To fight off the urge to cry, I keep myself busy by actually using the toilet, even though I didn't really need to go. And I take a moment to stare at myself after washing and drying my hands.

"You can do this," I whisper to myself. "They are home."

Shit. I'm making myself worse, so I splash some water on my face and dry it off, taking in a steadying breath.

When I unlock the door and open it, a chest comes into view, and before I can even assess what's going on, I'm shoved back inside and cramped in as Elliot closes us both in.

"What are you doing?" I snap, my arse right up against the sink.

"What do you think I'm doing?" He grins down at me, his hand working to undo his jeans.

"You can't be serious. You want to... right here... now?"

When he smiles, I nearly melt.

Elliot has the most brilliant smile. It's one of those smiles that lights up his whole face. It's rarely seen though, and I'm helpless to do anything but bend to his will when he gives me this brief glimpse.

"I can't stop thinking about your cunt, Ell."

"It's not like you to give in and let yourself have something you want," I point out, and his smile falls.

"Maybe I've changed."

I shake my head. "Nope. You held back at the club. You haven't changed."

"Maybe I'm just fucking horny. It's either you or Margie."

I scoff, my grin wide as I hitch my dress up and start working my panties down.

"Well Margie can't have you." I shoot him a wink, and a slight smirk returns to his lips. "You gonna come inside me?" I ask, and a growl rumbles in his chest.

"I'm gonna fill your cunt, Ella. It'll be leaking out of you for days."

I fist his shirt and tug him down until we are nose to nose, practically breathing the same air, and I lean in, parting my lips to kiss him.

In an instant, his hands are gripping my hips and spinning me, facing me to the mirror, and as our eyes meet in the reflection, he frowns, and spins both of us, so I'm facing the back wall above the toilet.

"Brace the shitta," he commands, and I'm still bloody reeling from what just happened.

He kicks my feet wider, shoves up my dress, exposing my arse and fists his hand in my hair, bending me over the damn toilet.

I'm grateful it has a lid, and that this luxurious plane actually has a nice bathroom, but this isn't how I pictured this going.

"Elliot, wait."

"Don't talk. Just hold on," he snaps, almost like he's angry... at me.

Before I can open my lips to argue with him, the head of his dick glides through my folds, coating him in my wetness, and then he finds my entrance and surges in.

A strangled sob falls from my lips as my tears start to come, and I don't even understand why I'm crying other than the fact that something with Elliot feels off.

There was no foreplay. He didn't even let me kiss him. And now, this is the third time he's been inside me since buying me, and it's from behind, once again.

"Fuck. You're so wet," he grunts, thrusting hard and fast, and I don't even know how I'm wet other than my body is a bitch and doesn't give two fucks about my heart.

I can't respond because I'm crying, and I'm trying like hell to hold it back so he doesn't notice. I don't want to make him feel bad. This is a *me* problem, right?

And hell, maybe I deserve this level of cold conduct from him. Maybe it's just a glimpse of what's in store for me.

Hell, maybe I misunderstood my role in coming home with them. Luey and Joel did say I had to be available to them wherever and whenever they wanted.

Their fuck toy.

Elliot's hips slap against my bare arse as he pounds me like he hates me, and normally I love this level of rough brutality, but right now, my heart and body are in different places.

And that's the problem right there. My heart shouldn't be getting involved when it comes to sex with these men.

"Fuck. Yes." He pistons, his fingers digging into the flesh on my hips, so biting I think his fingernails break my skin.

With his other hand still fisted in my hair, he tugs on it with each thrust, causing burning at my roots, and I can't help but cry out, which he must mistake for me coming, because he speeds up, lost in some sort of frenzy only he's a part of, and three thrusts later, he's jerking, stiffening, and grunting as he spills inside me.

My knuckles turn white as I hold myself up over the toilet, my tears creating small puddles on top of the lid, and this time, I'm grateful I avoided makeup today. They like seeing my black tears, but perhaps I simply don't want to give that to them anymore.

"Fucking best pussy around." Elliot groans as he pulls himself free, and for a moment, I don't feel like Elliot is here in the room with me. I feel like it's Joel when he's furious, and Luey when he's being spiteful. Not gentle Elliot. Not the only one who ever understood what I went through as a child.

This isn't him.

I feel him cleaning himself up behind me, but I don't dare move. I don't want him to see my face. See the tears he caused. And lucky for me, he has no intention of making this personal, because he gives my bare arse a slap, snickers, and leaves me alone in the bathroom.

16

Joel

Something is off with Ella. Ever since she got on the plane, she's been quiet. And after coming back from the bathroom, she moved to sit in the single seat across from Margie and started drinking.

Ella never used to drink on account of her alcoholic old man, and given the way Margie frowned when Ella poured herself a glass, I have to fucking assume she hasn't been much of a drinker over the last eight years either.

The other strange thing is Elliot. He's usually quiet, but right now, he's fucking chatty. Like he's been drinking or something. But I haven't seen him have anything but the coffee at Ella's this morning.

Luey keeps shooting me wary glances, clearly noticing the shift too, and fuck, I realise it's entirely possible Elliot took something.

But fuck, it's been years since he used. Has he really fallen off the fucking wagon?

After three glasses of that girly shit, Ella falls asleep, her head resting against the window. But Margie remains awake, her gaze always watchful over Ella and Coby, who is also asleep, drooling on Luey's arm.

Since now isn't the time to ask Elliot if he's taken something, I relax back and endure his chattiness for the remainder of the flight, feeling fucking exhausted by the time we land in Newcastle.

The moment the plane touches down, Ella startles awake, and I bite back a smirk as she quickly wipes up the trail of drool on her chin.

I fucking love her drool. Especially when it's from my cock invading her mouth.

Her eyes instantly flick to Coby, making sure he's okay. He's awake now too, ooohing and ahhing over things out the window, and Luey chats away with him, like they are old friends... Or father and son.

The thought has my gut fluttering, and fuck, that's a weird sensation. My gut isn't the fluttering kind. Not at fucking all.

After the plane pulls up at the private hangar, we stand and start moving off, and Ella quickly inserts herself behind Coby, taking his hand, her eyes avoiding not just Elliot's, but mine and Luey's too.

Martel, having got off the plane first, gets the luggage as we make our way to the people mover SUV that feels more like a compact limo with the back seats facing each other. Ella gets Coby buckled in and takes the middle seat next to him, while Margie takes the seat next to her, leaving the three of us on the other row of seats.

I study Ella as we drive. The way she talks quietly with Coby, pointing out things as we drive past them, and how she successfully manages to not look at either me, Luey, or Elliot for the entire forty-minute drive from the airport.

When we drive down the street of Luey's house, she falls quiet, no longer chatting with her son, her shoulders tensing, her fists balled and knuckles turning white as she stares out the window.

I bet she never thought she'd be returning here.

Is she scared right now? Or excited?

Nah, definitely not excited given the way her knee starts jiggling the moment we slowed to turn through the gates of Luey's house.

"Is this a hotel, Mummy?" Coby asks, and finally, her whiskey eyes flick to us.

"No," she breathes, dragging her gaze back out the window. "This is where Luey lives."

Coby beams, his wide eyes shooting across to Luey.

"Wow. You must be rich."

Luey chuckles, but doesn't say anything, and I frown, darting my eyes his way.

His mouth is tense, and he turns his eyes out the window this time, completely avoiding the answer.

"This is your home now too," Elliot interjects, gaining Coby's attention, and his big eyes widen as they shoot up to Ella.

"Is it, Mummy? Can we live here?"

Ella's smile is strained when she glances down at her son, but instead of nodding, she shrugs.

"We'll see, buddy."

The fuck.

I thought we'd been through this already.

The car pulls to a stop outside the mansion, and we all pile out, Luey giving instructions to Martel and Dougal, his other driver slash assistant, before leading the way inside where Tula, the house manager and cook greets us.

My eyes trail Ella's every move. From her fierce grip on Coby's hand, to the way she keeps a wide berth between them and us. To her wide eyes, taking everything in, committing it all to memory.

The house hasn't undergone any major changes in the last eight years, so I wonder if being back here is making her want to run again.

Given her tense shoulders, I'd say, probably.

"Tula, please show Ella, Margie, and Coby around and get them settled in their rooms," Luey orders, and Tula, the sixty-year-old loyal servant, nods with a pleasant smile, gesturing to the staircase.

We watch them take each step up, Coby's little voice never stopping, a million questions falling from his lips, but not a single one answered as Ella remains quiet.

"In the den. Now," Luey snaps at both of us, and I want to headbutt him for getting fucking pissy with me, since I didn't do anything, but I follow Elliot into the den and head straight for the single malt, pouring myself a decent splash.

"What the fuck is going on?" Luey snarls, closing the door, and I glance up to see his glare firmly set on Elliot.

"You mean the fact that in a matter of hours, we found Ella," Elliot scoffs, "fucked her, tried to kidnap her, and found out she has a kid to one of us? Because fuck, I don't know how to feel about any of this."

"Not what I'm talking about," Luey snarls, and Elliot's eyes narrow.

"What the fuck else is more important that that? Like, for fucking real, man, one of us is that kid's biological father. Not to mention we've missed what? Seven or eight years of his life."

"He has a point," I mutter before taking a sip of the scotch. "I kinda wish your old man was still alive so I can pound my fist into his smug fucking face. He fucking took not only our girl, but our kid away from us too."

Luey cringes, and fuck, I feel bad for bagging his dead father, but this shit isn't fair. Elliot is right. We missed seeing our kid smile for the first time, and say his first word. Take his first fucking steps.

Fuck. I feel sick, and my eyes instinctively shoot to Henry's vacant cracked leather chair. The one Luey now uses to run the multiple businesses from.

"I feel the same guys. Trust me. I'm fucking reeling at the news of Coby, but right now, we have a more pressing fucking concern." He turns his glare to Elliot.

"What the fuck have I done?" Elliot snaps. "Aren't we talking about Ella?"

"I'm not talking about Ella. We'll get to her in a minute." Luey strides forward, reaching out and gripping each side of Elliot's face and leaning in to get a look at his eyes.

"Get the fuck off me!" Elliot shoves him back, his wild eyes shooting to me. "What the fuck is going on?"

"That's what we'd like to know, Elliot."

His eyes narrow and his lip curls. "I don't know what the fuck you're talking about."

Luey huffs. "You haven't fucking shut up for the last five hours. What have you taken?"

Elliot flinches back like he's just been slapped, his frown deep, and when his gaze flicks to me, it's filled with hurt. Betrayal.

"You arseholes think I'm on something?" he snaps, jabbing a stern finger at both of us. "What? Can't I just be in a fucking good mood? Can't I fucking feel happy without it being related to getting fucking high?"

"It's out of character, man," I admit, even though I hate having to say it.

Elliot scoffs. "I can't believe you two." He throws his arms up in disbelief. "Did you ever stop to think that I'm fucking excited for life for the first time in eight years because we got our Ella back? That couldn't possibly be it, right? Any lick of happiness, and I must be fucking using again."

"This isn't you, happy." Luey steps forward, gripping Elliot's shoulders as he keeps his voice low and even. "This is you spiralling."

For a long beat, Elliot doesn't speak. He just stares into Luey's eyes.

"I'm not wrong," Luey adds.

"Well, maybe a lot is happening." Elliot shrugs Luey off him and moves to the desk, leaning his arse onto it. "I didn't think we'd ever see Ella again, let alone find her, fuck her and discover we have a fucking kid. Or at least one of us does." Elliot shrugs, shaking his head. "I'm fucking clean, man. You know I never want to go back to that..."

"You really didn't take anything?" I ask, and his angry eyes snap to me.

"Fuck no."

Luey and I collectively sigh as we stare at our mate, but his admission only makes me more confused about everything that happened... or didn't happen on the flight.

"Why was Ella so quiet on the flight?" I ask, and Elliot frowns.

"What do you mean? She was sleeping."

"She fell asleep after polishing off three glasses of champagne, something she never used to do," I hiss through gritted teeth, the frustration of the situation starting to get to me. "And that happened after she came

116

back from the toilet. You know, when you said you were going to check in on her and see if she was okay?"

"What happened in the toilet?" Luey steps closer to the desk like he's preparing to catch Elliot if he tries to run.

"What do you think happened?" Elliot snaps, crossing his arms over his chest.

"You fucked her." Luey comes right out with it, and Elliot shrugs.

"Yeah. So?"

"Was it consensual?"

Elliot's eyes widen at Luey's question before anger flares to life over his face.

"Of course it fucking was!"

"You sure about that?" I ask. "Because something clearly happened during that visit to the bathroom that left our girl fucking quiet and withdrawn."

Elliot frowns, his gaze dropping to the floor as he thinks.

"She didn't fucking say no," he murmurs, no anger in his tone this time.

"Did she say yes?" I ask, and his eyes snap to mine.

"She pulled her own fucking panties down. That seems like a fucking clear yes to me."

Hmmm, that's true. Why would she do that if she wasn't into it?

"Then what the fuck's going on with her?" Luey huffs, flopping back into the armchair.

Elliot shrugs, and for a few minutes the three of us are quiet.

I sip on the scotch, embracing the warm burn that trails down to my gut with each sip.

We got on the plane, and she seemed fine. We took off, and she seemed fine. She excused herself and went to the bathroom... and when she came back, she wasn't fucking fine.

Something happened in that bathroom.

Elliot fucked her. She removed her own fucking panties...

My eyes flick back up to Elliot. "Did she come?"

He frowns, his dark gaze meeting mine. "Of course she did... at least, I think she did."

"You don't know?" Luey sits taller in the chair, his glare locked back onto Elliot.

"I was a little fucking busy," Elliot snaps.

"Did you kiss her?" I jump in and ask, and his glare darkens as he shakes his head.

"No."

"Eat her?" Luey asks, and again, he shakes his head.

"Finger her?" I ask.

"No!" Elliot snaps.

"Give her clit any fucking attention?" Luey stands from the chair with a snarl.

"No."

"The fuck is wrong with you, man?" I snap, nearly spilling the scotch when I over-gesture towards him.

"She was wet as fuck," Elliot snarls. "She was into it."

"Probably leftovers from us earlier, you idiot." Luey huffs, tossing his hands up, his palms slapping the sides of his legs when they come back down.

"Fuck..." Elliot frowns, his panicked gaze darting from Luey to me. "Do you think I hurt her?"

"Did she moan?" I ask before downing the rest of the scotch in one gulp and placing the glass down on the side table.

"She made a noise... maybe a gasp." Elliot shrugs.

"Anything else?" Luey asks, and again, Elliot shrugs.

"I don't fucking know. I told you I was busy."

I huff out a laugh, but there's little fucking humour in it. "You used her."

"What?" he chokes out, the panic in his gaze growing.

"You fucking used her," I repeat. "You went in there, didn't give her a lick of fucking attention to even prepare her for your cock, and fucked her without making sure she at least came first."

"The fuck!" Elliot shoves forward off the desk, getting all up in my face, and I fucking take it, my lip curling as we butt foreheads. "Don't act like you two didn't fucking use her in the shower."

"We were reminding her of what she's been missing." Luey's hand comes between us and urges me back. "Trying to make sure she got on that fucking plane, but we fucking made sure she came. More than fucking once, you selfish prick. Fuck, she probably thinks as soon as she got on that plane, everything changed."

"Fuck," Elliot whispers, staggering back.

"Yeah, fuck," Luey grunts, turning his back on both of us as he starts to pace.

"Position?" I ask, and Elliot stiffens.

"What?"

"What position did you fuck her in?" I press.

"None of your fucking business." Elliot lurches forward, fisting the front of my shirt, and once again, we are forehead to forehead.

"It *is* our fucking business," I seethe. "She's ours. *All* of ours. What fucking position did you fuck her in?"

He shoves me back, anger contorting his face as he answers. "The usual, alright?"

"Fucking hell, Elliot. You need to go back to your therapist," I yell, ready to punch the fucker.

"The fuck for?!" he yells right back, looking like he wants to punch me with that balled fist by his side.

"You've been fucking chicks from behind since the day Ella left us," I point out, hoping like hell my words fucking sink in. "And now she's back, you can't even fuck her face to face like you used to? She's not one of the whores you see!"

A gasp has the three of us stiffening, our heads snapping to the now open door, and fuck me, standing right there, having heard God fucking knows how much of this fucked up conversation, is our Ella, mortification etched across her face.

J'ELE

17

Ella

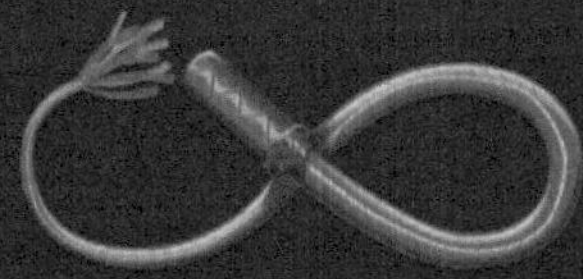

Oh my God! I wasn't just imagining it. Elliot really fucked me like that because he can't bear to look me in the eye while he does it.

"You really can't look at me while you..." Tears flood my eyes as my heart splinters inside my chest.

"Ell..." Elliot steps forward, but I hold my hand up to stop him.

"How many?"

"What?" he asks, confusion furrowing his brow.

"How many girls... whores have you fucked that way?"

"Ell—"

"How many?!" I screech, my control snapping.

"Fuck... I didn't keep a headcount." Elliot rakes his hand through his hair, making it stick up at the back.

"A lot then," I snap, and he snaps right back.

"Yeah. A fucking lot."

I knew they all would have been with other women, just like I've been with two other men, but this... knowing Elliot's pain ran so deep that he hasn't shared a single real moment with another woman, and then treated me the same way. It hurts. But I was the one who left, right? Maybe I deserve his coldness.

Even so, it doesn't make hearing it any better. God... the way he fucked me in that bathroom.

"You fucked them all from behind?" I ask, but my tone is still snappy.

"So what?" He closes himself off by crossing his arms over his chest and turning his back on me, pacing towards the window.

"Why?" I whisper, but it's loud enough for him to hear. For them all to hear.

Elliot just shrugs, but Joel answers for him.

"So he didn't have to see their faces."

Elliot doesn't deny it, his back still to me, as he focuses on whatever is out the window.

"Elliot?" I slowly approach him, and he grunts in acknowledgement. "I want to hear it from you."

"Fine." He spins, his wild eyes locking with mine, tears glistening his dark orbs. "You want to have this conversation? Then let's have it."

I flinch back a few steps as he stalks me, and he only stops when Luey's hand slaps his chest to stop him from taking another step.

"You fucking left, Ell. You left a fucking note saying you couldn't do this. No other explanation. You were just gone. We couldn't find you anywhere. It was like you vanished without a fucking trace." He throws his hands up in defeat. "What was I supposed to do? Never fuck anyone else again? Because I wouldn't have if I had known why you really left. And I wouldn't have if I had known we'd get you back. But I can't fucking change the past, and when you left... Fuck!"

Elliot spins away, his voice cracking with the emotions flowing from him, and I'm about to step forward to go to him when he turns back, shaking his head.

"In the beginning, I fucked whores. Only whores. Women I could pay to avoid any fucking emotional attachment, and I fucked them from behind so I could... pretend they were you." He takes a moment to clear his throat, his eyes dropping to the floor as my tears spill over. "So fucking sue me for pining after you, Ella." His eyes flick back up to mine. "You fucking broke my heart. I did what I had to do to try to fucking survive it."

"I didn't want to leave you," I whisper on a sob, and his face softens as he steps forward, reaching out to cup my cheek, his thumb swiping away some of my tears.

"But you did, Ell. You left."

"You know why." I lean into his palm, so warm against my skin.

"Yeah, I do now." His hand drops to his side, leaving me feeling cold and alone. "But I didn't then. I can't go back and change how that made me feel anymore than you can change the fact you left."

We stare at each other for a few long beats, the only sound in the room is the ticking clock on the wall.

"But you're still angry at me," I say quietly, and Elliot shakes his head.

"I'm not angry with you. I'm just angry."

Shit. I totally get that. I've been that way for years too.

Nodding, I bat at my tears, taking in a deep breath to work up the courage to be honest.

"You hurt me today... in the bathroom."

His face falls, and I immediately want to take the words back, but I can't, and I shouldn't. We need to have this conversation. Secrets have kept us apart for too long.

"Not physically," I blurt, needing that to be clear. "I can take your brutal fucking, Elliot, but you were so lost in yourself... you didn't hear me say, *wait*. You didn't hear me crying. You didn't pay me a lick of attention. All I was, was another body for you to fuck." I step forward, taking his hand in mine as the pain of what I just said contorts his expression. "And I get it. You have shit to get right in your head, but I didn't agree to come here to be treated like that."

I drag my gaze from Elliot to Luey, and then to Joel before dropping Elliot's hand and taking a step back.

"So unless you can treat me right, this shop is closed."

A strangled sound falls from Joel before he steps forward. "You know I treat you like a goddess, baby."

"I'd never be unfair in the bedroom with you, Ella. You know that." Luey remarks with a frown, but his words, and Joel's, aren't enough.

Glancing back at Elliot, I see him visibly gulp, and I ask him what I really need to know.

"Can you look at me when you... fuck me?"

He stares at me for a long moment, his whiskey eyes dancing between mine before he shrugs... and my heart sinks.

"Then until you can," I pause to swallow the lump of emotion clogging my throat. "Don't come near me."

18

Luey

Yesterday was a fucking shitshow. I don't know why I thought we'd get her back here and everything would go back to the way it used to be. Fucking dumbass, I guess.

After the confrontation in the den, we gave her space to settle in with Coby and Margie, who seems to be hitting it off with the house staff.

I feel guilty as fuck though.

I lied to Ella... big time. I'm starting to think it was a bad fucking idea, and I don't know how she will ever forgive me when she finds out.

And she will find out. It's been a part of the plan for the last few years, and more so after I found out just how fucking low my old man would sink to get what he wants.

But fuck we gotta get this over with. Despite the shit that went down yesterday when we arrived home, I've gotta rip the fucking bandaid off and tell her the truth.

"Do you think Martel and Tula can handle Margie?" Ella asks from behind me, and I turn to see her looking over my shoulder at where Margie leads Coby out to the pool house where they are having a movie night and sleepover.

My staff have strict instructions to not come to the house until we give the all clear. We need time and privacy to get through tonight. Lies and secrets have ruined our lives for well over eight years. Now it's time to put them all to rest and move the fuck on.

"I think I might need to give Tula and Martel a pay raise, but yeah, they can handle her." I grin down at Ella, and she offers me a half smile.

"I hope you don't think you're going to wine and dine me and my panties will magically fall off so the three of you can fuck me."

A laugh bursts from me at Ella's words, and I shake my head.

"I wouldn't dare think of it, Ella." I reach out and hook my finger under her chin, tilting her head back so she keeps her eyes on mine. "But I need to discuss a few things with you... and the guys. I don't want any disturbances until we get a few loose ends tidied up."

"Okay," she practically whispers, and I give her a reassuring smile despite the dread churning in my gut, releasing her chin and gesturing to the dining room.

Following her in, we find Elliot and Joel already there sitting at the table, and Joel pats the chair next to him, his excited eyes soaking in the pretty red dress hugging Ella's curves.

Fuck. Red is the perfect colour for this evening.

She offers Elliot a smile, but it's strained, and I hope like fuck that after tonight, they get closer again.

He's gonna need her support, and so will Joel.

They will need each other.

"This looks nice." She comments on the fancy place settings before she frowns, her eyes falling to the extra place.

"Uh... If Coby and Margie aren't gonna be here then why is there an extra place set?"

She's too fucking perceptive.

"It's for our guest," I tell her, catching Joel's wary look.

He's worried about tonight. About how Ella will react when she finds out.

"Guest?" Ella frowns. "Who's coming?"

Elliot sighs, dropping his eyes to the table, and fuck, he's going to make her flee with anxiety with that reaction.

"You'll see." I smile as fucking warmly as I can. "I'll go and get our guest."

Even though Ella doesn't stop frowning, Joel makes small talk as I leave the room, moving quickly through the house, down to the basement.

I've always hated coming down here, but the last couple of years I've had to more often.

Stepping inside the concrete room, my eyes fall on the man in the chair, a black hood covering his head, just as I asked Martel to do.

"I've been waiting years for this day to come," I say, moving to the chair and loosening the ties, helping him to blindly stand.

His muffled voice mutters incomprehensible words on account of the tape over his mouth, and I take his arm in a biting grip, leading him from the room, and up the stairs.

He keeps trying to speak, so I clip him over the head and snarl towards the black hood. "Shut the fuck up or I'll kill you right fucking now."

He quietens, shuffling along as I lead him, and as I approach the dining room, my heart races with what's about to happen here.

Will it scare Ella away?

Will it scare Elliot and Joel away?

Will it drive a wedge between us all, or will it bring us closer together?

For a moment, I consider turning around, but I need this. They need this, so I take in a deep breath and lead him around the corner and into the dining room.

A loud gasp escapes Ella when she sees me leading a man into the room, her eyes going round, yet a thousand questions dance across her expression.

"What's going on? Who is this?" Ella squeaks, and the man in my hold starts grunting, obviously knowing whose voice that is.

Joel and Elliot watch on, unsurprised, already well aware of the man I've been keeping in the basement. They don't say anything. They don't offer Ella any information. They just watch and wait, knowing shit's about to get real.

Only they don't realise just how fucking real it's about to get.

Shoving him down onto the chair at the empty place setting, I tie him to it, making sure the rope is secure before I glance back at Ella.

It's time for the truth.

The truth for everyone.

"I lied," I say, keeping my eyes on my girl, and her frown only deepens.

"Lied about what?"

"I told you my dad died," I say before dragging my gaze to the black hood, fisting the fabric and tugging it off his head. "He isn't dead yet, but he will die tonight."

JELE

19

Ella

A choked gasp flies from my lips as I leap up, my chair tipping backwards, crashing to the floor as my eyes land on Luey's father.

"Henry!" I screech, stumbling to the side, my mind already mentally counting the steps to the door.

Henry snarls, but the tape across his mouth muffles the sound.

"W-what's going on?!" I take another step to the side, edging closer to the door, even as my eyes take in the very man that threatened my life, and the life of my unborn child all those years ago.

He looks so much older than he did back then. Thinner. More dishevelled. And there are bruises... all over his face and arms. Some are yellow, like they are nearly healed, and some are black and purple, like they are new.

"I had to lie, Ella." Luey's voice draws my attention to him and the broad set of his shoulders as he stands tall and proud next to his frail looking father. "If I had told you he was still alive, my prisoner in the basement, you would never have come back with me."

"P-prisoner?" I choke out, and my eyes flick to the door.

I need to run. To get Coby and get the hell out of here.

They tricked me. They brought me back here to kill me. They have Coby, and I know they won't kill him, but they'll keep him.

Oh my God! Was Margie in on it, too? Is that why she moved here so willingly? Has she been working for Henry all this time?

Jesus H Christ. Of course she has. She just turned up out of the blue, asking about the room I had to rent, and it was like she was too good to be true, offering to pay rent and to help look after Coby so I could work.

"Don't fucking run!" Luey snaps, stepping away from his father and closer to me. "Take a moment to see what's really happening here, Ella. Henry is tied to the fucking chair. He's lost weight. He has scars and bruises. You are safe."

Safe? Is he serious?

My eyes snap to the doorway again.

How far could I get?

My gaze flicks to Joel and Elliot then, finding them relaxed in their chairs like Luey didn't just bring his dad to the dinner table wearing a hood and covered in bruises.

"I don't understand..." I trail off, a tension headache sliding into place, and I pinch the bridge of my nose.

"Elliot and Joel haven't understood either." Luey starts to explain, his gaze shifting to his mates. "They think I've kept Henry alive because he's my dad and I can't bear to kill him, but that's not why he's still breathing right now."

My brows shoot up, and I glance at Joel and Elliot again to see their confused frowns.

"I had to wait until the four of us were all together," Luey snaps, his glare practically burning a hole in the side of his dad's head. "Because I know *the* secret."

I stiffen, feeling a chill ripple up my spine.

"You mean... you knew about Coby all along?"

Joel growls at my words, and when I glance his way, his eyes aren't on me. No. His death glare is aimed straight at Luey.

"No, Ell-Bell. Not that secret." Luey ignores Joel and looks at me pointedly. "The *other* secret."

"The other..."

Oh.

Ohhh. Shit. Luey knows?

My eyes widen, flicking to Joel and Elliot to see them looking more confused than ever.

"That's right." Luey sighs, crossing his arms over his chest as he glares down at his father. "*That* secret."

"But... You can't... It will crush them. It will destroy this." I gesture from Luey to his two mates, but Luey simply shakes his head.

"I have to, Ella. They need to know." He clears his throat, his Adam's apple bobbing like he's struggling with his emotions. "They deserve the truth."

"What the fuck is going on?" Joel snaps.

"That's what I'd like to know. What fucking secret?" Elliot adds, but Luey doesn't answer, moving closer to his dad, who is grunting and thrashing against the rope that secures him to the chair.

"What's that, Dad?" Luey lifts his hand to his ear like he's trying to hear better. "I can't quite hear you."

Loud muffled yells rumble from Henry, before Luey snaps into action, gripping the corner of the tape covering Henry's lips, and tears it clean off.

"You no good bastard!" Henry snarls as soon as the tape is free. "You're a fucking idiot, son. What do you think will happen by revealing the truth?"

Another shiver ripples through me at hearing the voice of the monster that's haunted my nightmares for the last eight years.

"What I think, old man," Luey bends, getting in his father's face. "Is that they will finally get what they rightfully deserve."

Henry scoffs. "And what of you? You think they're going to keep you around out of the goodness of their hearts? Fucking unlikely!"

Luey shrugs, standing tall again. "Maybe they'll hate me, simply because you're my father. Maybe they'll kill me too. But at least they have each other again." Luey gestures from Joel and Elliot to me. "And they have Coby. You knew about him, right? Your grandchild?"

"So what? I have a grandson. Big fucking deal!"

Luey chuckles dryly, sounding way too similar to his father right now. "Don't pretend you didn't keep tabs on her over the years."

I stiffen when Henry shrugs.

Did Henry know where I was all this time?

"Lu! Enough with the fucking mind games!" Elliot snaps, standing from his chair. "What the fuck's going on?"

"They'll kill you," Henry mutters in Luey's direction. "You're a fool. I raised you better than this."

"They might take pity on me instead of killing me, but that's not on me or them. It's fucking on you!"

"I was protecting you, and now you're going to fuck it all up. If they don't fucking kill you, Louis, they'll fucking boot you. Watch how fast they turn their backs on you. You'll be homeless, living on the fucking streets."

Luey shrugs, crossing his arms over his chest again. "Then that's where I belong."

"You're a fool."

"I'm the son of a fool. That I'm sure of," Luey grunts, his eyes shifting to me, and then the others. "You all deserve the truth, no matter how hard it is to hear."

"What the fuck is the truth then?" Elliot grits out, his teeth clenched like he's barely containing his frustration.

"Will I tell them?" Luey asks, his gaze shifting back to Henry. "Or will you?"

I know this secret. It's what started all of this. The threats. The blackmail. It's the real reason Henry used my unborn child against me to convince me to leave and never reveal this secret.

Henry's lips thin like he's sealing them shut, and Luey scoffs out a hateful laugh.

"Fine, I'll do it, you fucking coward." Luey slaps the tape haphazardly over his father's mouth again, before turning his gaze to Joel and Elliot.

"This is all yours." His arms stretch out, gesturing to the room around us, and Elliot and Joel frown, looking even more confused.

"What the fuck are you talking about?" Joel snaps, and Luey's eyes soften, and I know he's thinking about what he's about to reveal to his best mates.

"Last year, I stumbled across a file Dad had been hiding. It was a flash drive, with a business agreement, and well..." His gaze flicks to me briefly, like he's gearing up to do one of the hardest things he's ever had to do... and I guess he is. "Long story short, my old man got weaseled out of the deal. You know the ones your olds were working on before they died?"

Even though Joel and Elliot are still frowning, they nod.

"Well, my dad told you the deal didn't go through, and that your parents died before it could, but he fucking lied."

Joel's face looks stricken. Like his mind has taken him back to the day he was told his parents died. I still remember his face. How lost he looked. How he broke right here in this very room, crashing to his knees as a guttural scream tore from his lips.

"Not only did the deal go through," Luey continues. "It was the reason both of your parents went on that trip, to celebrate and set up the new worksite. But the investors weren't interested in dealing with Henry. They considered him a snake, and that's a direct quote from one of the emails I found in the file. So the investors made a condition in the agreement that Henry not be involved. Not even as a silent partner. You can imagine how that went down."

Henry starts thrashing in the chair, his muffled yells clearly cursing his son out, but Luey ignores him, his eyes dancing between his two best mates.

"This fucker took matters into his own hands. He was already the trustee of your parents' wills, which also appointed him as your legal guardian should something happen to them. The only way he could access the riches, which he thought he was entitled to, was by becoming your guardian."

Luey leaves that bomb hanging in the air, and I turn to face Elliot and Joel as they just stare at Luey, like he's grown two heads.

"He couldn't have become your guardian unless your parents were dead. So he killed them," Luey rushes out, his voice cracking like he's trying not to cry. "Well, he paid someone else to do it, but they died in that helicopter accident because my old man arranged it."

Tears burn my eyes as I glance between the three men I ran from eight years ago. The very men I ran from, to not only protect my baby, but to protect their friendship.

Slowly, one by one, Elliot, Joel, and even Luey, turn their growing glares to Henry.

"You killed our parents?" Joel snaps, and Luey reaches forward again to rip off the tape so Henry can respond.

"I did you both a favour!" Henry yells, spittle flying from his lips. "Your dad would've spent it all on drugs anyway, Elliot. And Joel, your mum would have sent you away to boarding school. She already had the paperwork. I fucking kept you together."

Luey scoffs. "But you didn't, did you? Ella found the file, didn't she? When you had her do some clerical work for you over the summer. She found it, and you used what you'd found out about us and her pregnancy to force her away."

"You knew she would have told us." Elliot, who has been relatively quiet until now, seethes, his eyes wild with rage. "But threaten to kill her child, and you knew she'd leave to protect him."

"She is a whore. She would have torn the three of you apart anyway, spreading her legs like that for the three of you at once like she's the fucking star of a porn flick."

Elliot lunges for Henry, his fist crashing into his cheek with a crunching smack, nearly knocking the chair over with Henry in it.

"Don't you ever speak about our Ella like that again, you piece of shit!" Elliot bellows, his face red with rage. "I'll fucking cut your tongue from your mouth!"

"You don't have the fucking balls!" Henry snaps back.

Elliot goes to lunge again, but Joel wraps his arms around Elliot from behind, dragging him backwards to the other side of the room.

For a long moment, the only sounds in the room are Elliot's panting breaths, and the wheeze coming from Henry every time he breathes.

"I don't know if I'm Coby's dad or not," Luey turns to his mates. "But I love him. I love Ella. And I love both of you."

Reaching into his pocket, Luey pulls something out and places it gently on the table.

It's a set of keys.

"Everything you thought was mine, isn't. This house. The staff. The cars. The bank accounts. The businesses... they are actually yours." Luey bobs his head to Joel and Elliot before dragging his gaze to me.

"That's it. No more lies. You all deserve better. Ella and Coby belong here with you." Luey takes a step back, his venomous gaze regarding his father for a moment before lifting back to his mates. "I'll leave. Give you all some space. Let you figure out if and how I fit into your lives."

Then, before any of us can protest or respond, Luey pulls out a gun from the back of his pants, presses the barrel to Henry's temple, and pulls the trigger.

JELE

20

Elliot

A month ago, our lives changed. We found Ella. Learned we had a son. Brought them back here. Found out that Henry killed our parents. Henry died for real this time. And Luey left.

I'd been so in my fucking head about finding out the truth about my parents that I wasn't around when Luey had Martel help him clean Henry's brains off the carpet, table, and wall. They got rid of the body, and then, in the dead of night, Luey left.

Things haven't been the same since.

My reaction to finding out Henry was the one responsible for killing my parents was why I went and hid in my room for two fucking days. I felt bad that my reaction was thankfulness rather than grief or anger, like what Joel was going through.

My old man was an abusive alcoholic, and my mum was a prescription drug addict who preferred the high rather than anything fucking real. So yeah, I was kinda thankful that Henry killed them, but what I wasn't fucking thankful for was him chasing Ella off or keeping my son from me.

When I finally emerged from my room, Ella was sitting alone in the living room, staring into thin air while Margie played outside with Coby. And Joel... he'd turned to the bottle and spent his time trashing anything that reminded him of Henry.

I realised we needed to get our shit together and find Luey, so with Ella's help, we sobered Joel up, cleaned up the house and tended to some business that we've never had to deal with before, and set our sights on bringing Luey home.

The only problem is, Luey didn't want to be found.

Apart from Joel taking afternoon walks with Ella down to the beach, there's been nothing going on romantically or sexually between any of us. I've been trying to get closer to Ell, but she's been distant. She either misses Luey too much, or she's just not interested in pursuing anything with me again, and fuck if that thought doesn't rip my heart out.

After getting back from her afternoon walk with Joel, Ella excuses herself to go and get changed since she and Joel obviously had a splash fight in the waves given the trails of water splashes over her dress.

I give her a five-minute lead before making my way up to her room and knocking on the door.

My heart pumps faster as I hear her bare feet pad across the timber floors to the door, but when she swings it open, eyes wide and a smile tugging at her lips, only for it to drop when she sees me, my heart fucking sinks.

"Sorry... It's just me."

"Oh... I thought it was Coby." She shakes her head, forcing her frown to even out.

"He's playing snap with Joel," I explain, and she nods awkwardly. "Can I... come in?"

She bites down on her lip, considering my question, before nodding and opening the door wider to let me through.

It smells like her in here. Sweet. Fresh. Tempting.

"I'm sorry," I blurt, spinning to face her after I hear the door click shut, and her brows shoot up. "I'm messed up, but I'm working on it, Ell. I swear."

"Good." She nods, leaning against the door. "You need to, for yourself."

"I need you," I rush out, and worry flickers across her expression before she pushes off the door and grabs for the handle.

"I need to get back to Coby."

"Ella, please." I lurch forward, resting my hand over hers to stop her from opening the door, but the moment our hands touch, she snatches hers back, her tear-filled eyes locking with mine.

"I love you, Elliot. But I can't do this until you're really ready."

"Fuck, I am," I breathe, stepping closer to crowd her in, and press my forehead to hers. "I really fucking am. But you *need* to let me show you."

"How?" she whispers, like she's too scared to speak any louder.

"How do you think?" I grin, easing back a bit to study her beautiful expression.

"Sex," she states, and I nod.

"It's the biggest part of this, right?"

"It is but—" She stops herself and shakes her head. "No. It's not the biggest part. The sex part is a symptom of something bigger, Elliot. We can't just fuck face to face and think that will fix things."

"I know... fuck, I know. But here's the thing. The sex part is huge for me," I admit, stepping back and dropping my eyes to the floor as I fight the urge to bolt.

Suck it the fuck up, Elliot. Don't you fucking prove her right.

"I didn't want to have sex with anyone else," I admit quietly, fighting against the burn engulfing my throat and eyes. "But it was the only time I felt close to you, even though you weren't here."

Her delicate hand appears in my vision, reaching for my hand, and I let her take it, watching her thumb stroke over my skin as she tries to comfort me.

Fuck, her touch has the power to break me.

This was the view I always had. A hand. An arse. Long dark hair. I'd find chicks with something aside from their face similar to Ella, and I'd fuck them. It was always from behind, and I always focused on the one feature that reminded me of her.

Trying like fuck to swallow the tennis ball sized lump in my throat, I force myself to lift my gaze, travelling up the front of Ella's dress, over her curves until our eyes meet.

"We all dealt with losing you differently," I start to explain. "Luey focused on learning the ropes of his father's businesses while paying people to try and find you. Joel took to social media launching campaigns to hunt you down... but me... I just needed to feel you."

"You don't have to explain," she whispers as fat tears pop from her eyes, so I reach up, cupping her face and sweep them away as they fall with my thumbs.

"I need to, Ella. As hard as this is for me, it's how I heal, right? By facing my pain. By telling the truth."

A sad smile pulls at her lips as she nods into my hands, but I don't let her go. I can't bear the thought of not touching her right now.

"When we went out to clubs, I'd search the crowds for you. It was like I was wishing you'd appear out of thin air and walk straight back into my arms..." I shake my head at how fucking stupid that sounds now, and I drop my hands from her face, but she quickly links her fingers with mine, not willing to let me go. "The first time, I spotted a girl that had hair just like yours. Her face was completely different, and she was a little taller, but from behind, her curves and the way her dark hair brushed the top of her arse... in my head, all I could imagine was you. That you were there at that club. Dancing. Having fun. Eye fucking me."

The pain that flashes through her eyes fucking slashes through my heart.

The last thing I want is to make her hurt, but she needs this truth as much as I need to face it.

"So I took her to the stinky club bathroom, and fucked her up against the door, much the same way I did with you in the suite at the Mask House." A shudder rolls through me remembering that first time with someone else.

I knew it wasn't Ella. My brain, my fucking body knew, but my anger controlled me. It made me stay and see it through. It forced me to keep my eyes locked on her hair. On the way I had it wrapped in my fist. Just like I used to do with Ella.

"There were so many, Ell," I choke out, feeling like I'm about to fucking crack wide open. "But not once was I happy. Not fucking once. Not until the Mask House. Not until the plane. I might have taken you from behind because my head was messed up, but my body and heart fucking knew it was you. Every fucking thrust of my cock, Ell-Bell. I knew it was you and nothing else mattered in that moment."

"But on the plane, you were so cold towards me as you..." she trails off, more tears popping free.

"It was habit. That's all I can put it down to. I knew it was you, but also, I was fucking scared that it was you, because what if you break me again? I would never survive it."

A loud sob lurches from her lips as she throws her arms around my neck, and I fucking hold her so tight, breathing in her fruity scent, the muscle memory of it making me feel at home.

"I'm sorry," she cries, her breath shuddering before she speaks again. "I never wanted to leave you. Any of you."

"I know, baby." I give her a long squeeze.

We hold each other for a long while still practically pressed up against her door, and when I ease back to look down at her, I see all the pain in her eyes, so similar to mine.

"Y-you coded a g-game about h-hunting me," she sobs, and a grin tugs at my lips.

"I did. The guys helped and, well, it's not just about hunting you, Ell. It's about finding you, and claiming you."

Her lips part as her brows shoot up.

"There's sex in the game?"

"Well, the original game is fade to black, but there's a bonus game that costs a fucking fortune for players to buy that is all about us fucking you."

Her mouth falls open in shock. "There is not."

I chuckle, nodding. "There fucking is. I'll show you later."

"Oh my God, Elliot. Is that even legal?"

"It's rated R, baby. But it's legal."

A giggle slips from her, and she slaps her hand over her mouth as she shakes her head.

"I feel like I should be more mortified."

"Let's see how you feel after you play it. I bet you'll end up all hot and bothered."

She smirks at that, reaching up to dry the tears from her cheeks.

"I don't know if you've noticed. But I'm always hot and bothered around you guys."

I grin, and press my forehead to hers again, needing to be fucking close.

"Do you see now? It's always been about you, Ell. Everything is because we love you." I lean in a little closer, feeling her breath fan over my lips as I talk, my chest rising and falling with anticipation. "I only ever wanted more moments with you, even though the way I did it is fucked up. But I'm here with you now, and I don't want to focus on just your hair, or your hands, or the curve of your fucking hot arse." I fist my hand in her hair, pulling back just enough that she can see the truth in my eyes. "I want to look into your beautiful eyes as I move inside you. I want to watch you watch me as you come. I want to be with you fully in every moment from now on."

Even as another sob lurches from her lips, I swallow it by claiming her lips.

She opens for me, accepting my tongue and sucking on it like she's desperately missed it, and fuck, the little moan that falls from her mouth and into mine has my cock rock hard.

I fist her hair tighter, as my other hand presses to the small of her back, keeping her flush with me as the kiss deepens.

It's a long, slow and fucking sensual kiss that has me dipping her back in my arms, and fuck, she melts into me like she fucking belongs there.

"Stop," Ella pants, shoving at my shoulders to put a few inches of space between us, the action bringing us eye to eye. "Show me."

"Now?" I grin, knowing exactly what she means, and she nods quickly.

"Please."

She doesn't have to ask me twice.

Releasing an animalistic growl, I sweep her up in my arms and carry her to the bed, toeing off my boots before dropping her onto the mattress.

"Strip, Ell-Bell. Don't leave a fucking stitch of clothing on."

Her lips part as her eyes flare with heat and desire, and she quickly gets naked, while I do the same.

I came prepared with a toy, because one of the things Ella and I used to experiment with was sex toys. It's actually how we had our first sexual encounter together.

Well, I kinda walked in on her using the handle end of her electric toothbrush to get herself off, and well... I asked if I could watch. Shit got real fucking heated from that point on.

"I have something for you," I tell her as she leans back on her mattress, her eyes trailing down the front of me, and now I'm happy I've been doing sit-ups every morning lately.

"Oh? Is it six inches long and hard as a rock?"

I frown. "I think you mis-spoke, Ella. Don't you mean eight inches?"

A laugh bubbles from her lips before she smothers it and nods. "Yes, that's totally what I meant."

Dramatically rolling my eyes at her, I reach for my pants and pull out the toy I stashed in my pocket.

As I hold it up before her, those whiskey eyes widen with curiosity, and her pretty cheeks flush.

"What is that?"

I give it a shake, and the long, thick tongue-like part of it wobbles up and down.

"It's a tongue fucker." I grin, and those dark brows shoot up.

"A tongue fucker?" She shifts forward, more than curious, and I know bringing her this gift was a good idea. A bit of an icebreaker to get past the awkward shit I've somehow managed to insert between us after she found out I had an issue with taking her face to face.

I turn the toy on, showing her the different actions the silicone tongue can do.

"Imagine a tongue long enough to go alllll the way inside you, licking and flicking, all while this part sucks your clit." I point to the part that aims for the clit.

As excited as she looks about this toy, it doesn't stop her smile from falling.

"But I thought... Aren't you going to..." She shakes her head in frustration.

"It's a gift, Ella. Just like the old days." I hook my finger under her chin lifting it so she can't look anywhere else but at me. "Let me start again by doing the things we used to do. Let me show you how good it'll make you feel before I fuck you."

For a long beat her eyes dance between mine, like she's trying to figure out if I'm actually going to go through with it.

She shouldn't worry, but I get it. I fucked up on that plane. I need to earn her trust again.

"Okay," she breathes, and my fucking shoulders relax.

Fuck. I didn't realise how tense I was.

I spend the next few minutes tying her to the bed, because that's also our thing, and we slip into the roles we used to play so easily, it's hard to believe that it's been over eight years since I've been alone in a bedroom with her like this.

Once her ankles and wrists are cuffed and secure, starfishing her on the mattress, I hover over her, watching how she trembles ever so slightly.

"Cold?" I ask, and she shakes her head. "Scared?" She shakes her head, but then shrugs as best she can in that position.

"I'd never hurt you, Ell-Bell."

"You wanted to hurt me at that club."

My eyes darken at her words, and I lean closer, our skin searing as it touches, our breaths mingling.

"I didn't want to hurt you in the way you think. I had considered some edging and orgasm denial, but fuck, Ella, never anything sinister."

Her eyes turn glassy, so I lean in and press my lips to hers, reminding her that I'm here. I'm present. I want to see her face, kiss her lips, get lost in her stare as we fuck.

It's only seconds before she's moaning and I'm kissing a trail from her lips, down her neck to her plump tits, sucking her nipple deep into my mouth.

Her back arches, and I splay my lips so far apart I nearly choke on her nipple as I try to fucking devour her tits.

In seconds, my hands are replacing my mouth as I travel over her navel, down to her mound, and the needy little thing tries to chase my mouth with the lift of her hips as I hover over her core and blow air onto it.

"Fuck, Ell. You have the prettiest cunt."

"More." She practically begs, so I fucking give it to her, using my hands to press her thighs further apart as I glide my tongue up through her slit.

Her taste explodes on my tongue, and I turn ravenous, sucking her clit, lapping up her slickness, and dragging my tongue all the way down to tongue her perfect puckered arse.

She's writhing, struggling against the binds that hold her in place, desperate for more as I tease her.

Deciding to give her what she wants, I reach for the tongue fucker and turn it on, holding it to her clit for a moment before easing it deep inside her.

"Elliot!" she cries, arching, her hips thrusting as the long, thick curved tongue flicks her most sensitive parts inside, and I line up the sucker, easily finding her swollen clit, and attaching it.

I scoot back a little, still holding the toy in place as I watch how it sends her into a desperate frenzy, my cock fucking aching to bury deep inside her, but I fucking hold that back.

It can wait. I can wait. This is all about Ella right now. Not me.

A strangled cry surges from Ella's throat, and she explodes in seconds, clear fluid jetting from her cunt as she sprays all over the end of the bed.

"Fuck, Ell. That's so hot," I growl, leaning down to catch the last bit in my mouth before I start lapping up every fucking drop.

I remove the toy, and she shudders with each pass of my tongue, completely at my mercy, and completely trusting me to treat her right.

Fuck.

She's perfect.

Shifting back on my haunches, I give my cock a few long pumps, watching her chest rise and fall with panting breaths as she tries to calm down.

"Looks like you won't be sleeping in here tonight." I smirk, and her lips kick up at the corners.

"If I didn't know better," she pants, "I'd say you did that on purpose."

I throw my head back laughing. "Maybe I did."

"Untie me?" she asks, and I shake my head.

"Not yet."

"But—"

I shake my head. "Not yet. I want to fuck you like this. I want you to trust me completely... just like you used to."

"But I do."

"Then let me do this."

She nods at me, and I shift between her legs, fisting my cock and steering it towards her slick opening.

For a moment, I hesitate, my eyes focused on her pretty cunt.

Everything in me is screaming to keep my eyes on it. Don't look at her face. Don't look at those stunning eyes that have the power to destroy me.

But I have to. I need to. I want to be with her completely.

My eyes flick up to meet hers. "You ready?"

She nods. "Please. I've missed you so much."

I can do this. Just watch her beautiful face.

As I hover there, my tip pressing against her opening, I wait for the panic and dread to hit, but it never comes. All I feel is safe.

Home.

That's all I need to know, and without another thought, I surge in.

I've missed her too. So much. I went to some really fucking dark places when she left, and fuck, if it wasn't for Luey and Joel, I'd probably be dead right now. But those fuckers, they are more than my mates. They are family, and they pulled me out of the dark hole I was in, and helped me learn to live again.

It wasn't perfect. I was far from happy. But I was functioning.

Until now.

Fuck.

"I love you," I rasp as I thrust in and out, leaning close to hover my lips over hers.

"I love you too, Elliot. Always. I never stopped for one second. Not even when I thought you guys were gonna kill me."

With a growl, I claim her lips, punching into her, the walls of her cunt squeezing my cock like a fucking vice in the best kind of way.

She kisses me with desperation, and I taste her tears as we fuck, her cries getting swallowed with every pass of our lips.

Fuck. I want to feel her hands on me. I want to feel her claw the fuck out of me like she used to.

That thought has me fumbling for the cuffs on her wrists, and I somehow, blindly get them off, and the second I do, she gives me exactly what I want.

Her fingernails, just like claws, scratching into my flesh, and I just know she's drawn blood. Right in this moment, I know there's nothing in this world that will ever keep me away from her again, and as she starts to spasm around my cock with her climax, my balls tighten, and fucking ecstasy rushes through my nuts as I stiffen and explode deep inside her cunt.

And fuck, I can't help but think... I hope I just got her pregnant.

21

Ella

My heart flutters as Luey walks into the room, wearing blue jeans and a black button-down shirt. My fingers grip the chair by my legs as I force myself to stay in place, not wanting to seem too desperate. Too eager.

But shit. I've missed him so much.

After weeks of the guys begging him, Luey's finally coming back, agreeing to move into one of the guest rooms and pay board from the new job he got selling houses.

Of course, Joel and Elliot have drawn up papers to give him an equal share of everything they own, but they are going to sit on that information for a bit, knowing he might leave again, because if there's one thing we know about Luey, it's that he doesn't like charity.

Since moving back here, and Luey leaving, things have been tense, but still felt positive. Like we are all moving in the right direction.

I get why Luey left. He'd been carrying the secrets of his dad too, just not as long as me, and he blamed himself for his father's actions.

The thing is, Joel and Elliot never blamed Luey. Hell, they weren't even angry that he kept it from them. They were just happy Luey was the one to fix it.

Joel and Elliot aren't selfish men. They don't care for all the riches now at their disposal. The only thing they care about is this unorthodox family, and keeping us all together.

I feel for Luey though. The things he's had to do by locking up his own father. By beating him. By carrying that burden for so long. It's why he needed to leave as much as giving the guys some space to wrap their heads around everything. Those invisible scars will plague him for a long time, I'm sure, but at least he has us. We'll lift him when he's down, because that's what you do for the ones you love.

Margie has taken Coby to the city for the night, staying in one of the apartments the guys own, giving us the night alone so we can reunite properly, but Coby will see him in the morning.

He's been asking about Luey every day, and they've spoken on the phone a couple of times, although I'm not sure Luey wanted to hear how Coby's T-Rex sunk to the bottom of the pool, but still, he listened and asked questions, fully engaging with our son.

I'm sure Luey will hear all about the most recent dinosaur drama tomorrow, but for tonight, we need the place to ourselves. Not just me and Luey, but the guys and Luey too.

In anticipation of tonight, I've foregone panties. They will just get in the way and are entirely unnecessary for tonight's proceedings.

I've been aching for days leading up to this, playing the guys' game online with each of them, getting through the hunt, and then accessing the game which is basically porn. I mean, it's fun, and I had to tend to my own needs a few times, but it's nothing like the real thing, and I'm desperate to get back to that.

Luey's dark eyes lock on me as he takes a seat across the table from me, and I smile, feeling the blush creep up over my cheeks.

"You look beautiful, as always, Ella."

My smile widens, and Joel chuckles, taking the seat at the head of the table where Luey used to sit. Then, everything falls quiet.

"Uhhh, what do I have to do to break this tension?" Elliot asks. "This is not like us."

He's right. It's not.

I guess everyone is feeling a little off kilter given the power exchange now that Luey isn't the king of this castle.

I can tell he doesn't care, but Elliot and Joel do. I can tell they feel like imposters.

"Lu?" I ask, licking my lips, and biting them when his dark gaze tracks the movement.

"Yeah, Ell?"

"Would it be alright if I came over there and kissed you?"

His smirk is wicked, and he gives me a single nod, so I stand, shooting a quick smile at the other two.

Then, I lean forward and lift my knee onto the table, pulling myself up to crawl across to him.

His brows shoot up as the other two laugh, and the closer I crawl, the darker his eyes turn.

Reaching him, I lift my hand to his stubble, something that I've never seen him wear, but fuck, it makes him all the hotter, and I scrape my nails through it.

"Hey." I breathe.

"Hey." He grins, reaching up to weave his fingers into my hair. "Get those lips over here now."

I don't wait. I give him exactly what he demanded.

The moment our lips meet, he tugs me down off the table and into his lap, and I straddle him, feeling the hard rod of his cock under his pants.

I grind over him a few times, and his grip in my hair becomes biting, right before he tugs my head back.

"You're such a good fucking girl, Ella."

I beam. "Sometimes, I'm bad."

He growls, and Joel and Elliot snicker, knowing Luey's control is hanging by a thread.

Pressing my hand to Luey's chest, I push myself back, rising off his lap, and glance up to find all eyes on me.

Well... isn't this nice.

Moving to the opposite end of the table as Joel, I strip out of my dress, completely baring myself to them and soaking in the rumbles that fall from each of them in approval.

"Please tell me you're the main course, Ell-Bell." Joel beams, and I nod, moving to my chair to pick up the black leather strap.

When I hold it up, their smiles fade, and they watch every second of me collaring myself.

"I belong to you, Joel," I breathe, and he stands quickly, his chair scraping back as I turn my gaze to Elliot. "I belong to you, Elliot."

Another growl rumbles from him as he slowly stands, rearranging his dick in his jeans, and then I turn my gaze to Luey.

"And I belong to you, Lu."

"Yeah, you fucking do." He thumps his fist on the table, standing, before moving his hands to his fly, where he starts to free himself.

"Get on the table," Joel orders, and well, I'm not going to argue with that, I get back on the table, shoving off the plates that were in the centre.

Within seconds, lips and hands are on me, pinching, grazing, kissing, nipping.

Each of them kisses me, all four of us naked on top of the huge table, and the moment Joel fists his hand into Luey's hair and kisses him too, well shit, I've never been more turned on in my life.

A frenzy comes over all of us. I can't keep track of who's kissing me, or who's kissing who, and by the time my cunt is filled with Luey's cock, my arse stretched with Joel's long rod, and my throat is gagging around Elliot's girthy dick, I know that there will never be anything more meaningful, more beautiful, or more real that when the four of us come together and love each other in the most humanly way possible.

Luey, Joel, and Elliot were put on this Earth to be mine, and I to be theirs, but mostly, we are all here to be here for our little boy, Coby. The guys can be hard men, but they were born to be fathers, and I can't wait to tell them that they will be fathers again soon.

For the first time in years, my chest feels light, my heart feels full, and I can finally breathe.

THE END

Want another short smutty book with a dash of plot?

**Check out
SINFUL DESIRES
A spicy hidden identity workplace romance
novella**

READ FOR FREE
by joining my newsletter
HERE
OR
Read at a discounted price on
**KINDLE EBOOK
https://geni.us/sinfuldesires**

Sarah JD's Books

READ MORE BY SARAH JD

https://sarahjdauthor.com/books

Stalk Sarah

Want to join the conversation about your fav characters?
Join my Facebook Readers Group
SARAH'S VICIOUS KITTENS

JOIN HERE!
https://www.facebook.com/groups/
sarahjaneduncanreadersgroup

For more information on books & book
signing events please visit:
https://sarahjdauthor.com

SCAN
ME
STALK ME

Sarah JD

Sarah JD, also known as Sarah Jane Duncan, is an Australian dark romance author living her best life with her high school sweetheart, Mr Duncan.

Sarah can be found in her writing room plotting out her next smut filled romance, packed with angst, violence, and themes so dark you should probably question why you love it so much.

Sarah enjoys torturing her characters. There's nothing easy about their stories. They are hard, gritty, and painfully heartbreaking at times. But what doesn't kill us makes us stronger, right? And when you throw in a swoon worthy guy, or an alphahole you just want to slap, but also fall to your knees and obey, it's the recipe for a rollercoaster ride.

So buckle up. Read the warnings. And let yourself get lost in the dark stories Sarah creates.